FATE

Brings a Warrior

FATE
Brings a Warrior

Frank W. Edwards

For information, permissions, or other inquiries, contact:
Frank W. Edwards, Author
www.frankwedwards.com

ISBN: 978-1-970798-06-7
Cover design: Frank W. Edwards
Printed in the United States of America
First Edition

Dedication

To my parents, Frank and Elizabeth Edwards, whose warmth, wonder, and unwavering love shaped my youth. Without them, this book—and the journey behind it—would not exist. They remain forever a part of who I am and all I strive to become.

Contents

Chapter 1

The Battle of France and Dunkirk

★★★ They believed they had time. In the smoke-filled halls of the French military high command, maps were pushed across long mahogany tables with the confidence of old men who had already fought their great war and expected the next to look the same. Alongside them, their British counterparts sipped strong tea and circled Belgian defensive positions with wax pencils, comforted by the decades-old belief that trench warfare, attrition, and fixed fortifications would once again decide the fate of Europe.

In truth, the fate of Europe had already shifted—quietly, surgically—in the minds of men like Major Ernest Warnecke.

Warnecke stood at the edge of a makeshift command tent outside Trier, his gray field tunic dusted from the ride in. His face, angular and sharp like the mountains of his Silesian youth, wore a fixed calm. Beside him, General Erwin Rommel gestured to the terrain model with a commander's precision. The rest of the staff leaned in. Warnecke didn't need to. He already knew how it would unfold. He had seen it before.

Years earlier, under the burning Spanish sun, Warnecke had served as a junior officer attached to the Condor Legion. There, in the chaos of the Spanish Civil War, he watched cities collapse not from siege but from speed. In Toledo, he saw how columns of mechanized Nationalists pierced Republican defenses in a single day, while airstrikes turned resistance pockets into tombs. The screaming civilians, the scattered books of shattered libraries, the smell of chalk dust and cordite—those memories remained. He remembered a girl clutching a doll on a church step, eyes wide and unblinking after a Stuka bomb had silenced her village.

It was not just a war. It was a revelation.

And now that revelation was being made flesh.

The first attempt to stop the Germans after the fall of Poland began on paper—in the minds of Allied planners who believed their Maginot Line would hold and that the Germans would charge head-on, as they had in 1914. They thought the war would slow into another siege of mud and steel, where numbers and endurance would prevail.

But the Germans did something no one expected.

On May 10, 1940, as Allied troops surged into Belgium to meet what they believed to be the main German thrust, Army Group A, including Rommel's 7th Panzer Division, surged through the Ardennes—a forest the French generals had written off as too dense for armor.

Warnecke's eyes narrowed when they reached Sedan. The Meuse River crossings would be critical. As the Panzers reached the east bank, he observed the engineers methodically building pontoon bridges under artillery fire. By May 13, the German armor had forced its way across.

Behind them, France's fixed fortifications were irrelevant. In front of them, chaos reigned. By May 20, the German spearhead reached the Channel coast near Abbeville, slicing the Allied armies in two. The British Expeditionary Force, along with French and Belgian divisions, was trapped in a pocket along the northern coast, their backs to the sea.

Rommel's advance was so swift that even Berlin struggled to keep up. Communications lagged; commands came late. But Warnecke knew the tempo had to be preserved. Momentum was the weapon. And now, that momentum drove the Allies to a desperate choice—Dunkirk.

From the vantage point of a ridge near Saint-Omer, Warnecke raised his field glasses. Below, he saw smoke curling into the gray sky—not from burning tanks, but from oil reserves set ablaze by retreating forces. Beyond the haze, along the waterline, tiny figures swarmed the beaches like ants—thousands of them. British, French, Belgians, some armed, many not, all desperate to escape.

The air was filled with contradiction: the low thrum of patrol bombers circling above, the occasional staccato burst of machine gun fire from distant emplacements, and in between—silences. Long, aching silences, broken only by the cries of wounded men, the barking of orders lost in the wind, the moan of tides slipping over bodies in the surf. The scent of seawater mixed with oil and the sweet rot of abandoned rations.

Warnecke lowered the glasses and exhaled. "This will be their only victory," he muttered to no one in particular.

Rommel stood nearby, arms crossed, studying a field map that was already out of date. His expression held no glee, only calculation. He had seen victories won and squandered. He had lived through the arrogance of command.

He turned to Warnecke.

"We should press the attack," he said. "Now. Before they regroup."

Rommel's voice carried the clipped certainty of a commander who believed momentum could break nations. He spoke with the confidence of a man whose armored columns had already rewritten the rules of war across France and the Low Countries.

France, with its fog and villages, offered no such purity.

But Warnecke knew what was coming. The Halt Order, issued from Berlin under pressure from Göring and cautious high command, paused the armored advance just miles from Dunkirk. The Luftwaffe would finish the job, they insisted.

It didn't.

Between May 26 and June 4, over 330,000 Allied soldiers were lifted from the beaches by a motley flotilla of destroyers, ferries, fishing boats—even private yachts. It was not a victory, but it was an escape. Warnecke watched them vanish into the sea.

Later, as the Reich celebrated the fall of Paris and the signing of the armistice at Compiègne, Warnecke sat alone outside his tent near Rouen, reading dispatches by lantern light. The victories were historic, but something gnawed at him. Not because the Allies had escaped—but because so many believed the war was over.

He had learned in Spain that victory without vigilance breeds failure. Already, whispers of Churchill's defiance floated across the Channel. The British would not sue for peace.

He took out a notebook, drawing a thin line from Poland to France, then across to Britain. He paused, and began to write: *The French were finished. The British would follow. The Americans? Still hiding behind oceans and neutrality—too cautious, too comfortable. No nation stood ready. No leader could match Rommel. Not yet.*

He closed the notebook and blew out the light.

Chapter 2

Bloodlines of War

★★★ In the aftermath of Dunkirk, while the world held its breath for Hitler's next move, a restless storm was gathering across the Atlantic. That storm wore pearl-handled revolvers, cursed like a stevedore, and believed that fear was a weapon to be wielded as precisely as a Colt 45.

The United States, still officially neutral, watched Europe burn from behind the shield of oceans and policy. But that shield shattered on the morning of December 7, 1941, when Japanese bombers struck Pearl Harbor. In the span of a single day, isolation gave way to fury. America was at war.

And war had always been General George S. Patton Jr.'s natural element.

General George S. Patton Jr. was not merely a soldier by profession—he was a soldier by blood, forged in a lineage steeped in the smoke of American battlefields. His destiny had been charted long before his birth on November 11, 1885, in San Gabriel, California, by a family whose very marrow carried the legacy of war.

The Patton family traced its martial heritage to the Civil War, where George's grandfather, Colonel George S. Patton Sr., had fought valiantly for the Confederacy. A man of stern conviction and battlefield gallantry, Patton Sr. met his end during the Third Battle of Winchester in 1864. But before his death, he had earned distinction at the very heart of the Confederate saga—on the blood-soaked fields of Gettysburg.

It was there, on July 3, 1863, that the elder Patton joined thousands of gray-clad soldiers in what history would come to call Pickett's Charge. His unit, part of the Confederate assault force that day, surged across open ground toward Cemetery Ridge under blistering Union cannon and musket fire. It was a desperate gambit orchestrated by General Robert E. Lee—a final attempt to break the Union lines and end the war with a Southern victory on Northern soil.

The charge failed. The Union line held. And though the name that would echo through history was that of General George Pickett, it was a host of subordinate commanders, including Patton's grandfather, who bore the weight of the doomed advance. In the years that followed, veterans and historians would refer to that moment as the "High Water Mark of the Confederacy," the peak from which the Southern cause would irrevocably recede. The tide of history turned on those few fateful minutes, and with it, a family legacy was cast in bronze and fire.

Young George Jr. grew up under the long shadow of that charge. Stories of valor and defeat were etched into the rhythm of his upbringing. His father, George S. Patton II, had never fought in a war but was a devout student of military history. He filled their home with tales of heroism, maps of battles, and relics of the Lost Cause. These were not bedtime stories—they were lessons in destiny. George Jr. absorbed them like scripture.

He was raised to believe he was part of a continuum, a reincarnation of warriors who had fallen in the past and whose unfinished glory awaited fulfillment. The ghost of Gettysburg was never far from his thoughts, nor was the obligation to redeem his grandfather's place in the annals of military history. He did not mourn the Confederate defeat—he studied it, sought to understand it, and promised himself that he would never repeat its mistakes. Where they had failed, he would triumph.

From an early age, Patton showed the marks of an old soul wrapped in a young frame. He read voraciously—Julius Caesar, Napoleon, and Lee—and began memorizing battlefield tactics long before he learned algebra. He attended the Virginia Military Institute briefly, following in his grandfather's path, before gaining admission to West Point, where the ideals of martial honor and unyielding discipline would harden him further.

There was a fire in George Patton that could not be extinguished. It burned for glory, for country, and for the ancestors whose dreams had died in the rolling fields of Pennsylvania. Every war he fought was a personal reckoning, a chapter in a much older saga. He carried the Civil War with him—not as a burden of shame, but as a standard of purpose.

Now, in this new war, far from the graveyards of Virginia and Gettysburg, Patton once again found himself commanding men into battle across the fields of Europe. But the ghosts followed him. He saw them in the eyes of young soldiers who looked to him for courage. He heard them in the rumble of artillery. He felt them at night when the wind shifted, and the smell of gunpowder hung in the air like incense over a hallowed altar.

He was no longer the grandson of a Confederate colonel. He was the inheritor of a fallen charge, the instrument of a new and righteous campaign. Patton would not seek redemption for the South—he would seek victory for America. But the blood of Cemetery Ridge still pulsed in his veins.

In his journal, Patton once mused that he believed in reincarnation, that he had fought in many wars before and would fight in many to come. Whether he truly believed it or not, those closest to him knew he walked with the dead. Not just his own dead—but all the dead. The dead of Bull Run. Of Antietam. Of the Marne. Of Verdun.

To follow General Patton was to march in the company of ghosts.

Chapter 3

The General in Motion

★★★ Patton was a cavalryman at heart, born into a legacy of warfare and honor. His jaw, perpetually clenched, looked hewn from Tennessee limestone. His eyes, a flinty blue, missed nothing. In late 1942, he arrived in North Africa not as a savior, but as a man who knew the stakes—and how little time there was left to prove America belonged on this world stage.

The American defeat at Kasserine Pass in February 1943 had stung like a slap to the face. Green troops, scattered leadership, and a lack of respect for German discipline and tactical superiority had resulted in a rout. Eisenhower needed order. He needed fear turned into resolve. He needed Patton.

Patton arrived in II Corps headquarters in a sand-blown, ill-kept village outside Tebessa. He stepped from his command car wearing riding boots, jodhpurs, and a scowl that seemed to darken the North African sun. Within hours, mess tents were inspected, uniform standards enforced, latrines dug to regulation. The entire corps snapped taut under his voice like a taut steel cable.

"Officers will wear ties. Enlisted men will shave daily. Discipline is the soul of an army."

The Germans, meanwhile, were no longer facing the disorganized Americans they'd embarrassed weeks earlier. When Patton struck, he struck hard—at El Guettar, the Americans held the line against German tanks with grim ferocity. The tide was turning, and Patton was at the helm.

But the prize was not just the redemption of American arms. It was Rommel.

On March 23, 1943, Patton's forces engaged what they believed to be the famed Desert Fox near El Guettar. The battle was a chess match in heat and dust. Tank shells screamed across the dunes, artillery roared like ancient gods. When the smoke cleared, it was Patton who stood victorious. It was said he took no joy in the win—at least not immediately.

Later, as reports trickled in, Patton learned that Field Marshal Erwin Rommel had not been present during the battle. An ear infection had forced his return to Germany days prior. Accompanying him was Major Ernest Warnecke, the same sharp-eyed strategist who had stood beside him at Dunkirk. Warnecke, loyal and analytical, had reportedly voiced concern over leaving the theater at such a critical moment, but Rommel's health and Berlin's insistence left little choice. Observing the battle unfold from afar, Warnecke recognized that Rommel's successor, General Hans-Jürgen von Arnim, had failed to execute the plan with the precision and aggression Rommel would have demanded. The positions were solid, the strategy sound—but the timing faltered, and the responses lagged. According to Warnecke's later assessment, the defeat was not solely due to Patton's tenacity, but also to a lackluster performance by German command. Warnecke was disappointed in the outcome and quietly embarrassed over the loss to Patton, believing that had Rommel remained, the battle might have ended very differently. In his place had been General Hans-Jürgen von Arnim, executing a plan crafted by Rommel before his departure. The German positions, the traps, the counter-maneuvers—they all bore Rommel's imprint.

Patton's aide, a thin-lipped West Pointer named Hugh Gaffey, broke the news with typical brevity.

"Sir, Rommel wasn't in the field. But this was his plan."

Patton stared out over the rolling sand where his tanks had broken through.

"Then I beat him," he said.

The words weren't triumphant. They were a balm. He needed to believe he could match the Germans not just in firepower, but in genius. Rommel had become his shadow opponent—an enemy he respected, even admired.

The victory opened the door to the next campaign: Sicily.

In July 1943, Operation Husky began. Patton was initially subordinate to British General Bernard Law Montgomery, whose Eighth Army was tasked with the main thrust through eastern Sicily. Patton, relegated to a supporting role, chafed under the arrangement.

Montgomery, with his beret, ramrod posture, and clipped Oxford diction, viewed Patton as a relic—brave, perhaps, but reckless. Patton saw Montgomery as arrogant, slow, and theatrical. Their relationship was a brittle truce, sustained only by the needs of war.

When Allied progress on the eastern flank bogged down, Patton took matters into his own hands. His forces stormed ashore at Gela, then raced toward Palermo in a whirlwind campaign that stunned both Axis commanders and Allied planners. Roadless terrain, German machine gun nests, mined passes—none of it stopped Patton's drive.

He arrived in Palermo three days ahead of schedule.

His men, dusty and sunburned, cheered him as he entered the city. Photographs showed him standing atop a command jeep, helmet gleaming, the American flag whipping behind him like a standard of divine vengeance. But Patton wasn't done.

He turned east, toward Messina.

What followed was a furious dash—a race to reach Messina before Montgomery, to prove American steel and strategy could outpace British caution. Patton's engineers rebuilt blown bridges overnight. Infantrymen marched until their boots bled. Artillery rolled on mule trains when trucks failed. On August 17, 1943, Patton's men entered Messina just hours before Montgomery's columns arrived.

He had won the race. But not the war of perception.

Beneath the triumph lay tension. Reports filtered back of civilian casualties in towns like Troina and Sant'Agata. Field orders had sometimes been ambiguous, their interpretations aggressive. And then, in a moment that would haunt his career, Patton entered a field hospital in Nicosia.

It was late July. The heat was a living thing, a beast that clawed at men's sanity. Inside the tent, Patton encountered Private Charles Kuhl, slumped on a cot, no visible wounds, claiming exhaustion and nerves.

"You're just a goddamned coward," Patton hissed, slapping the soldier across the face.

"Days later, near Nicosia, it happened again with another exhausted private."

Nurses were appalled. Doctors filed quiet protests. News reached Eisenhower, and soon, it filtered to Washington. In the salons of power and press rooms of New York, the tale of General Patton's outbursts became the latest controversy.

In public, Roosevelt stood silent. In private, Eisenhower seethed. He needed Patton's fire, but not his flameouts.

Still, the general remained indispensable. As the Allies turned their gaze to mainland Italy, Patton was shifted—officially reassigned, unofficially cooled down. He left Sicily under a cloud, but not in disgrace. His methods were questioned, but his results were undeniable.

As the Italian campaign began in earnest, and British forces clashed with German defenders along the boot, Patton bided his time. He studied maps in England, conferred with planners, and wrote in his journals about destiny, discipline, and duty.

He knew the big fight was coming. He could feel it in his bones.

And when it did, when the gates to Europe opened again from the shores of Normandy, he would be ready.

But first, he had to endure the weight of his own legend—and the waiting that followed his own storm.

He had slapped two soldiers.

But he was far from finished.

Chapter 4

The Shadow Before the Storm

★★★ Near San Stefano, Sicily – August 1943. The tent flaps cracked like rifle shots in the dry Mediterranean wind as General George S. Patton strode down the narrow aisle of the field hospital. Beyond the ridgelines, artillery still muttered across the island in uneven bursts, the sound rolling through the valleys long after each shell struck.

General George S. Patton moved through the hospital aisle with hard, deliberate steps. Medics straightened when they saw him. Nurses lowered their eyes. His polished boots, stained now with Sicilian dust, struck the wooden planks with a rhythm that sounded almost accusatory.

Rows of wounded soldiers filled the long tent. Some slept beneath morphine haze. Others stared upward with vacant eyes that seemed fixed somewhere beyond the canvas ceiling. The smell inside was suffocating—a mixture of sweat, antiseptic, blood, and damp wool.

Patton had walked through field hospitals before. France in the last war. North Africa only months earlier. He believed hospitals revealed the true condition of an army more honestly than any battlefield report ever could.

Then he saw the young private.

The boy sat hunched on the edge of his cot, trembling violently despite the heat. No visible wound. No bandages. No blood. Only pale skin and eyes that refused to settle.

Patton stopped.

"What's wrong with him?" he demanded.

A captain in medical corps khaki stepped forward cautiously. "Combat exhaustion, sir. Severe shell shock."

Patton's expression hardened instantly.

Shell shock.

The phrase disgusted him—not because he lacked courage himself, but because he believed courage could be demanded from others through force of will alone. To Patton, armies survived by discipline, aggression, and momentum. Fear was contagious. Weakness spread.

The private looked up, lips quivering.

Patton struck him across the face.

The crack echoed through the ward. Several nurses froze. Somewhere deeper in the tent, a man groaned in his sleep.

"You're a goddamned coward," Patton snapped. "There's nothing wrong with you that guts won't cure."

The private began crying openly now, humiliated before the entire ward.

Patton leaned closer, voice low and venomous.

"You hear artillery and lose your nerve? Men are dying out there while you sit in here shaking."

The attending doctor stepped forward carefully. "General, the soldier's condition—"

Patton wheeled on him instantly.

"His condition is cowardice."

Then he turned sharply and strode from the tent, leaving behind only silence and the fading sound of his boots outside.

It should have ended there.

But war had changed. Armies no longer fought in isolation from politics, newspapers, and public perception. Stories traveled now—through whispers, letters, correspondents, and wounded men returning home.

And days later, near Nicosia, it happened again with another exhausted private.

The second incident spread far faster than the first.

By the time Patton reached Palermo, rumors were already moving through Allied headquarters. Doctors filed reports. Officers exchanged guarded looks. Correspondents heard fragments of the story through hospital staff and enlisted personnel. Some dismissed it as battlefield temper. Others called it brutality.

General Dwight D. Eisenhower could not ignore it.

Patton received orders to report immediately.

The meeting took place inside a sweltering command tent outside Palermo. Maps covered nearly every surface. Cigarette smoke drifted beneath the canvas roof in heavy layers, trapped by the humid Sicilian air. A fan rotated uselessly in the corner.

Eisenhower stood near the operations table when Patton entered. Omar Bradley lingered quietly along the far wall, expression unreadable.

For several seconds, nobody spoke.

Then Eisenhower finally turned.

"You slapped sick soldiers," he said flatly.

Patton removed his gloves slowly. "I slapped cowards."

Bradley looked downward.

Eisenhower's jaw tightened. "Doctors diagnosed combat fatigue."

"Combat fatigue kills divisions," Patton shot back. "One man breaks, another watches him break, then another. Fear spreads faster than artillery."

"You don't get to decide medical policy by hitting enlisted men."

Patton said nothing.

Outside, a truck engine growled somewhere beyond the tent. Voices drifted briefly through the canvas before fading again.

Eisenhower stepped closer now, lowering his voice.

"George, do you have any idea what this looks like back home?"

Patton's face remained rigid. "I'm not fighting this war for newspaper editors."

"No," Eisenhower replied sharply. "You're fighting it for America. And right now, America is reading headlines about a general striking wounded soldiers."

The silence that followed felt heavier than artillery.

Patton stared at the maps spread across the table—Italy, France, the Channel coast. The war was expanding faster than anyone had imagined. Sicily would fall soon. Then Italy. Then eventually France itself.

And he knew he belonged at the center of it.

Finally, Eisenhower exhaled.

"I'm not relieving you."

Bradley looked up slightly, surprised.

"But you are being removed from frontline command for now."

Patton's eyes narrowed.

"For how long?"

"I don't know yet."

The answer hit harder than any formal reprimand.

Patton had built his entire existence around movement. Speed. Action. Pressure. Battle was the one place where he understood himself completely. Without it, the world became political, cautious, slow-moving—everything he despised.

"You need me," Patton said quietly.

Eisenhower met his gaze directly. "I do."

It was the truth.

No American commander inspired fear in the German high command the way Patton did. His victories in North Africa and

Sicily had already transformed him into something larger than a man. Aggressive. Unpredictable. Relentless.

Even the Germans studied him obsessively.

And that gave Eisenhower an idea.

Weeks later, after Sicily had largely fallen silent, Patton stood alone aboard a transport aircraft crossing toward England. The roar of the engines filled the cabin while gray clouds drifted below like torn wool.

He felt hollow.

Reports from Italy reached him daily. Other commanders advancing. Other generals shaping the war's next phase while he remained trapped behind the consequences of his own temper.

He replayed the hospital scenes repeatedly in his mind—not with guilt exactly, but with frustration. Part of him still believed he had been right. Another part understood the world no longer permitted commanders to behave as battlefield tyrants, regardless of results.

That realization angered him more than the scandal itself.

When he arrived in England, he expected obscurity.

Instead, he found deception.

The British briefed him inside a dim operations room outside London. Maps lined the walls. Intelligence officers moved pins across the Channel coast while cigarette smoke drifted beneath hanging lamps.

A colonel pointed toward Pas de Calais.

"We intend to convince the Germans this will be the primary invasion site."

Patton folded his arms. "And?"

"And we intend to use you to do it."

Inflatable tanks. Fake radio traffic. Phantom divisions. Entire armies constructed from illusion and noise. At first, the idea offended him. Patton believed wars were won by steel, blood, and violence—not theater.

But as the briefing continued, he began to understand.

The Germans feared him.

Not Bradley.

Not Hodges.

Not even Montgomery.

Him.

His reputation alone could alter enemy deployments.

That meant his greatest weapon was no longer command.

It was myth.

Later that evening, Patton stood alone outside the compound while rain drifted across the English countryside in thin silver sheets. In the distance, truck engines moved along darkened roads carrying equipment toward hidden assembly areas.

Somewhere beyond the Channel, Rommel waited.

And for the first time in months, Patton felt purpose returning.

Not as a battlefield commander.

Not yet.

But as something stranger.

A ghost the Germans could not ignore.

Chapter 5

The Pint That Changed the War

★★★ He had always been forgettable. And that was the point James Paulson—the name he'd worn like a well-fitted coat for the past three years—had cultivated his persona with scientific care. His wool cap always tugged just a bit too low, his spectacles faintly smudged, his overcoat the shade of soot and drizzle. His voice, when he used it, carried no inflection worth remembering. At the postal depot outside Southampton, he was as much a fixture as the crates he moved.

To most, he was a soft shape in the fog.

The postmaster called him Jimmy the Quiet. That suited him perfectly.

But his real name was Gert Volke, born in the Saxon hills above Dresden, where the mist rolled over pine and stone. Schooled in Königsberg, trained in the shadow-world of Hamburg's Abwehr annex beneath Wilhelmstrasse, Volke had been groomed not to stand out, but to disappear. When he arrived in England in January 1942, he wasn't just prepared—he was embedded. He drank bitters instead of schnapps, tracked cricket scores with practiced curiosity, and even bought war bonds at the depot to complete the illusion.

His English was flawless—save for a faint Midlands lilt that no true Midlander would question. That accent had taken months to perfect, tested in a dozen anonymous towns before Southampton became his post.

He had not expected tonight to matter.

The pub—The Golden Pipe—was packed. Smoke curled beneath blackened rafters. The air was thick with coal fire, damp wool, and the sharp tang of spilled ale. Candlelight flickered inside clouded hurricane lamps, casting every face in shifting oranges and browns. In the corner, a sailor—bandaged and flushed—belted out a bawdy verse of The Quartermaster's Stores, pounding the table as girls in scuffed heels shrieked laughter.

Paulson—Volke—sat alone beneath a yellowed recruitment poster, its edges curled from steam and age. He nursed his pint with mechanical slowness, watching, listening, never straining. In a room so loud with war-weary cheer, invisibility came easy.

Then he arrived.

"An American. Tall, broad, and already well into a long evening of pints. His coat hung open just enough to flash his rank stripes—whether by accident or arrogance, it was impossible to tell. His cheeks were blotched red, his step heavy.

His voice sliced through the pub like a bayonet.

"The damn Krauts are gonna be wiped out at Normandy," he declared, slamming his mug on the table.

The word dropped like a brick into still water.

Paulson didn't flinch. He took another sip, slower this time. But inside, trained instincts snapped to life. Normandy.

Not Calais. Not Brittany. Normandy.

The American rambled on, loud and unsteady—bravado soaked in bourbon. Around him, no one seemed to care. If they noticed, they chalked it up to another GI mouthing off.

The MPs arrived within minutes—two grim-faced men in olive coats. They moved with practiced irritation. One muttered an apology to the barman as they grabbed the American by both arms. A brief protest followed—slurred and incoherent—before he was dragged out into the Hampshire night.

The noise resumed. The sailor launched into a new verse. Girls lit fresh cigarettes with trembling fingers. The barman resumed his endless polishing with the same damp rag. The wave passed.

But Volke lingered.

To everyone else, he was still Jimmy the Quiet. But inside, the world had shifted.

Normandy.

He would not report it as fact. That would be reckless. But it was the strongest hint in two years. If the Allies were careless enough to let such a word slip—even in drink—it meant Berlin had reason to hope.

He would encode it tonight. Invisible ink, pressed into a letter addressed to a fictitious Aunt Harriet in Manchester. A coded phrase—innocuous on the surface—would flag the name. The letter would post tomorrow. If all went well, it would pass through Salisbury, then make its way into Berlin's hands by the weekend.

Volke adjusted his glasses. His heartbeat stayed steady. He had been trained not to leap at shadows.

But this was not a shadow.

This was sunlight breaking through.

He rose.

Coat buttoned. Pint drained. No one looked up as he stepped past a group arguing over bread rationing. He pushed open the door and stepped into the damp street.

Mist clung to the cobbles. Somewhere down the alley, a lorry rumbled to life. But Volke didn't look back.

No one followed.

No one ever did.

Chapter 6

A Girl on a Bicycle

★★★ Spring in Kent arrived with restraint that year. Not with fanfare or color, but with a weary kind of hope. Along the hedgerows, primroses blinked open in pale yellow, their faces tilted toward a sky uncertain of its mood—sometimes light with promise, sometimes brooding with cloud. A cool breeze slipped over the fields and freshly tilled soil, carrying with it the scent of earth, sheep dung, and chimney smoke.

The narrow road winding through the chalk hills southwest of Dover was nearly empty. Petrol was rationed, and the war had quieted much of the countryside. Far overhead, the faint hum of an RAF patrol plane seemed reluctant to disturb the stillness.

A young woman pedaled a weathered Raleigh bicycle along the lane, its chain ticking softly with each turn. Her dress—a modest blue wool number—fluttered just above her knees. A wicker basket rested at the front of the bicycle, lined with a wool blanket and a cloth-wrapped bundle. Her scarf was tied neatly under her chin. Her cheeks were pink from the morning air.

She rode alone.

To the casual observer, she was perfectly ordinary. A governess returning from market. A teacher heading to lessons. One of thousands of women whose quiet routines steadied the home front.

But Ellen Washburn was not English.

She had been born Elena Wache in Munich, the daughter of a clockmaker who taught her silence and precision. She studied literature and languages at the University of Munich, reciting Kipling and Browning with a practiced British accent before her twentieth birthday. When the Abwehr tapped her in 1940, she didn't hesitate. Loyalty to the Reich had been instilled early. But even deeper than loyalty was hunger—for purpose.

By 1943, she had it.

Her German accent had been ironed out through exhaustive training. She mimicked BBC broadcasts until her vowels softened and her consonants clipped with gentle precision. In Lisbon, a retired opera singer with a taste for treason finished her transformation. By the time she arrived in Kent posing as a language tutor, her identity was watertight.

Ellen Washburn. Age 23. Protestant. Orphaned in the Blitz. Native of Leamington Spa. Unmarried. Reserved. Helpful.

To the village of Lydden, she was quietly capable. She taught French to the grocer's children. She folded bandages for the Women's Voluntary Service. She read The Jungle Book aloud in the bomb shelter during raids. The vicar's widowed sister, with whom she lodged, often said Ellen had "a heart made for England."

Ellen smiled at that.

But she had other purposes.

As she crested a low ridge, her eyes caught a flicker of motion far below—a movement in the grass that didn't belong. She coasted to a stop and wheeled her bicycle off the road and down a narrow path flanked by budding ash trees.

The path was rutted and overgrown, the branches overhead forming a kind of archway. Ellen ducked her head and guided the bicycle forward until the trees opened into a wide meadow.

What she saw made her breath catch. Below, at least two dozen soldiers moved in practiced rhythm—driving stakes, adjusting ropes, circling hulking shapes. At first glance, it resembled an armored encampment. Tanks. Trucks. Guns.

But something was wrong.

One of the tanks wobbled in the breeze. A private stepped forward and re-secured a guide rope, patting the side of the tank like it was canvas—and it was. Another soldier hauled a truck axle across his shoulders like a broomstick.

Then it became clear.

Inflatables.

Tanks made of air and cloth. Trucks fashioned from tubing and tarpaulin. From the sky, it would look like a real armored division preparing to move.

But from here, it was theater.

She crouched behind a thicket and watched. Soldiers hammered stakes into the soil and tied off lines to bulging shapes. One worked a hand pump into the belly of a deflated "Sherman," its side caving in like a sagging balloon. Another adjusted painted wheels beneath a wooden "lorry." From the air, it would be real. On the ground, it was illusion.

She reached into the basket and unwrapped a small leather case. Inside: a Kodak 35 camera—smuggled into Britain months ago under the pretense of being a gift from an American boyfriend.

She wound the film.

Click. One frame. Then another.

She moved slowly, adjusting her angle, keeping the ash branches between her and the clearing. Her training held. No wasted movement. No sound. Each photograph captured another layer of deception: inflated half-tracks, fake artillery, men moving with rote discipline under the gaze of command.

She paused on one shot—a "tank" with its side collapsed, a corporal crouching beside it with a hammer, as if fixing a shed.

It was absurd. But it was working.

Ellen lowered the camera and wrapped it carefully again. She brushed her skirt clean, wheeled her bicycle back to the lane, and pedaled on as though she had stopped to check the chain.

The photographs would go to her contact in Folkestone—a tinsmith who trafficked in more than metal. From there, they'd travel by courier through Ireland, then Spain, and eventually reach Berlin, sealed in a diplomatic pouch marked Hydrological Surveys: Southeast Coast, Spring 1944.

By week's end, they would rest on Field Marshal von Rundstedt's desk.

Ellen would return to Lydden. She'd correct spelling exercises, stir lentils for supper, attend the blackout drill. She would smile when the vicar spoke of peace. She would read from Kim to calm the children.

And not once would her voice betray what she had seen.

No one would suspect.

No one ever did.

She only hoped Paulson—quiet, gray, invisible Paulson—had found something equally useful. Because if the Allies were building this scale of illusion on the southeast coast…

Then the real invasion was happening somewhere else.

She didn't need to know where.

But she knew this: if Berlin believed what these fields of canvas suggested—

Then everything might depend on a girl with a camera and a man with a pint.

Chapter 7

The Ghost Army's General

★★★ Rain fell in slow, steady sheets over southeastern England, beading on the windshield of the Dodge command car as it rumbled toward FUSAG headquarters. Lieutenant General George S. Patton sat rigid in the passenger seat, jaw clenched so tightly it ached. His long, double-breasted trench coat shielded him from the cold, but not the deeper chill of disuse.

He had crossed deserts, driven tanks across two continents, and stood at the gates of victory. Now, he commanded shadows.

Officially, he was the head of the First U.S. Army Group—FUSAG. In truth, it was an army of illusions. Trucks made of plywood. Tanks filled with air. Aircraft that would never fly. A command built to deceive, not to fight.

The Dodge pulled into a hedgerow-shrouded compound that looked more like a supply depot than a headquarters. Rows of Quonset huts stood among camouflage nets and wooden sentry posts. Patton stepped out into the drizzle, boots striking gravel with purpose. Even here, among ghosts, he carried himself like war was just over the next hill.

Inside the operations tent, the air buzzed with rain on canvas and the rustle of maps. Colonel Oscar Koch, Patton's longtime G-2, handed over a freshly decoded intercept from Bletchley Park.

"They've bought it," Koch said, tapping the page. "Berlin references Calais directly. They believe the build-up's real."

Patton scanned the communique. The corner of his mouth twitched into something close to a smile. "Let them keep believing."

He folded the paper, slower now. The weight of it settled in.

"The thing about ghosts, Oscar," he said, "is they don't bleed. But the boys at Normandy will."

Koch looked up from the map table. "You don't think it'll hold?"

"It'll hold," Patton said. "Long enough, maybe. But even the best lie costs someone, somewhere. Just not us. Not yet."

Outside, another truck rolled past—its flatbed stacked with inflated artillery tubes, painted and convincing from the sky. Two soldiers performed a pantomime of unloading crates while a third photographed the scene for German consumption.

Everything here was part of the deception. Every visible movement, every leak, every signal. Operation Fortitude South wasn't just a feint—it was a masterpiece of misdirection, crafted by the British and reinforced by Patton's reputation. His very presence lent it weight.

Radio transmissions buzzed nightly with fake orders. Double agents like Garbo whispered "truths" to Berlin. Even aerial photos taken by Luftwaffe recon showed what the Allies wanted them to see: a massive invasion force gathering across the Channel from Calais.

Patton had become the keystone of the illusion. He toured dummy airfields. He gave speeches to units that didn't exist. He let himself be seen, be rumored, be feared—while Montgomery prepared for the real landing hundreds of miles west.

At night, alone in his quarters, Patton sat in silence. He had never feared battle—but irrelevance, that was another matter. Sicily still burned in his mind: the victory, the slap, the fallout. He had outrun Montgomery to Messina and then been sidelined by scandal. Now Monty commanded men. Patton commanded props.

But if the ruse worked, if the Germans held back their Panzers from Normandy for just a few days too long—then this charade would save thousands.

That was the calculation.

Even smoke could blind, if you poured it thick enough.

One evening, Patton stood alone on the cliffs above Dover. The wind whipped at his coat, tugging at the brim of his helmet. Across the Channel, Calais lay shrouded in haze and German concrete.

Beside him, Koch joined quietly. "They've moved another Panzer division north. Toward Boulogne."

"They're chasing ghosts," Patton said.

"They're chasing you."

He said nothing.

The wind howled. The Channel below churned like a great gray machine.

"They still think you'll lead the real invasion."

Patton finally turned. "Then let's give them a damn good show."

By early June, nineteen German divisions had been drawn north, away from Normandy. Even after the Allied landings, Berlin hesitated—convinced Patton's force would strike later, across the narrow straits. Hitler believed it. Rommel doubted. Rundstedt questioned. But still, the myth held.

Patton never fired a shot in Operation Fortitude. And yet, his absence did more than most battalions.

He was a warrior used as a weapon.

He had been forged in fire.

Now, he fought with smoke.

Chapter 8

Listening to Ghosts

★★★ The safe house in Buenos Aires was not much to look at—gray stucco stained by rain, its windows shielded by rusted bars and dusty blinds. A cracked mosaic tile in the entryway bore the faded outline of a sun, once golden, now pale as ash.

Inside, the air was stale with the scent of old cigarettes and paper. It was a listening post—one of dozens scattered across the globe under names no ledger would acknowledge. Argentina, with its port authority riddled by sympathizers and neutralist sentiment, had become fertile ground for silent wars.

The woman at the desk was neither old nor young. Her cropped brown hair, streaked lightly with gray, was tucked beneath a knitted cap. She wore no perfume. Her sweater was rough wool. Her name in this place was Teresa Avila.

It was not the name her mother had given her.

The headphones cupped her ears, thin wires snaking to a series of dials and patch cables glowing orange beneath the control board. The receivers were tuned to a frequency used by U-boat command in the South Atlantic, though Teresa doubted they'd pick up anything significant tonight. Most of the chatter had gone dark after spring. Signals were rarer now—and faster.

But tonight, something pinged.

A click. Then a slow build of static, followed by a series of numbers spoken in mechanical cadence.

Teresa straightened.

She lifted a pencil and began transcribing on a worn pad of graph paper. The voice, clipped and precise, repeated the sequence. It was German, female, and monotone—a numbers station transmission, likely masked inside weather data or maritime alerts.

But Teresa had been doing this for too long not to know when something shifted.

The sequence was long—too long for a routine broadcast. And buried in the final repetition was a phrase she had never heard before. "Jagdlicht bei Ebbe." Hunting light at low tide.

She blinked. That wasn't a code. That was poetry.

And poetry, in intelligence work, was a scream.

She removed the headphones and turned to the second receiver, tuning quickly. It clicked, fuzzed, then settled.

On another frequency—a different voice. Male. Also German. A shorter message, much tighter formatting. But then the call sign: Flammenvogel. Flame bird.

Her pencil hovered. The two transmissions weren't linked by format or frequency, but by tone—by temperature. She had no way to confirm yet, but this wasn't background noise. Someone, somewhere, had triggered a cascade. Maybe from Lisbon. Maybe from London.

She rose and crossed to the narrow desk where a wall map of Europe hung beneath a row of pinholes. A dozen red markers ringed the Channel. Five around Calais. Three around Cherbourg. One—only one—at Normandy.

She didn't place another pin.

She didn't have to.

Instead, she reached for the cipher pouch, unlocked it with the sequence etched into memory, and began encoding the transcription. Her message would go out to Buenos Aires Station, routed through Mexico City and into Madrid. From there, it would reach the listening desk at Abwehr command within the hour.

She worked quickly, methodically, aware of the ticking clock.

Downstairs, a dog barked once. A car door slammed. Then silence.

The war was everywhere and nowhere here. Some nights, the house was silent for hours. Other times, there were knocks on doors that never opened again.

But tonight, she didn't feel fear.

She felt certainty.

Someone had cracked something. A signal slipped through the noise. A whisper that, when passed through enough filters, might become a shout.

She finished the message, resealed the pouch, and paused before sending.

On the table beside her, beneath a chipped ashtray, lay a clipping from a British newspaper—smuggled in via diplomatic pouch, dated three days earlier. A headline read:

"Patton Tours Dover Encampment – Allied High Command Continues Build-Up Along the Channel"

A lie. Clearly.

But still, the photo had caught her eye.

Patton, back stiff, arm raised in salute, a general's baton in hand. Behind him, rows of tents. Of trucks. Of tanks.

But she saw the smudge just left of frame. A shape buckling in the wind. Canvas.

Teresa clipped the article for a reason. Now, with tonight's transmission, she understood why.

The deception was working.

She slid the encoded message into the transmitter and activated the circuit. The needle jumped. A hum filled the room. The data burst out into the ether—riding waves of static and intention, of fear and mathematics.

In the distance, thunder rumbled over the Plata.

Teresa Avila returned to her chair.

And somewhere in Berlin, a staff officer would soon be reading a ghost's report—sent by a woman who didn't exist from a house that never was.

Chapter 9

The Weight of Truth

★★★ Washington, D.C. – May 1944. Rain whispered against the windows of the White House Map Room. A single banker's lamp cast a greenish hue over the long conference table. The air inside was stale with tobacco and the smell of worn leather chairs, and the clock above the door ticked in stubborn defiance of urgency.

General Dwight D. Eisenhower leaned over the map of Western Europe, its edges curling from use, the surface littered with thumb-tacks and penciled arrows. A red grease pencil traced the coast of Normandy, circling five beaches. Beside it, a black arrow pointed north—to Calais.

Franklin Roosevelt sat opposite, his cigarette holder tilted between his fingers, unlit. The President's eyes were tired, the skin around them folded like parchment. The polio had wasted much of his body, but not his mind, and certainly not his grasp of timing.

"I'm not asking if it will work," Roosevelt said softly. "I'm asking if it will cost."

Eisenhower hesitated. The truth was heavier than he wanted to admit. "It will cost plenty," he said. "But if we don't draw their armor to Calais, Normandy becomes a slaughterhouse. We need the German high command to commit its reserves in the wrong place. Fortitude is our best shot."

The President nodded. "Patton's ready?"

"As ready as anyone who's been sidelined, insulted, and used as bait can be."

Roosevelt allowed himself the faintest smirk. "He always did love theatrics."

"Which is why it works," Ike said. "They believe in Patton. Fear him. Berlin reads every movement he makes like scripture. If they think he commands the spearhead, they'll double-down at Pas de Calais."

"And the real spearhead?"

Ike tapped the red-circled beaches. "Here. June fifth or sixth, weather permitting. Montgomery leads the ground component. Bradley and the Americans come ashore here—Omaha, Utah. The Canadians at Juno. Brits at Sword and Gold. Airborne drops inland, bridge seizures, roadblocks. But the risk—"

"—is everything," Roosevelt finished.

Outside, thunder rolled across the Potomac.

The President lit his cigarette and drew a long breath before exhaling toward the ceiling. "I remember Wilson, after the Somme. Eyes hollow. He said it was like watching men drown in mud, endlessly. I don't want that again."

"You may not have a choice."

"I know," Roosevelt said. He looked down at the black arrow pointing to Calais. "But I'll be damned if I let ghosts write the headlines while real men die."

He stood slowly, using the edge of the table for support, and made his way to the sideboard. The bourbon there was modest by presidential standards. He poured two glasses, handed one to Ike.

"To smoke and steel," Roosevelt said.

Eisenhower raised his glass. "And to the men who won't live long enough to know which was which."

They drank.

Silence filled the room again.

A knock at the door interrupted the quiet. Harry Hopkins stepped in, his frame thin and stooped, eyes sunken but alert.

"Sorry to intrude, Mr. President," he said. "Message from London. Confirmed receipt from Lisbon—coded intercept. The Germans are reinforcing the Channel line. Boulogne and Calais both. Nothing shifted to Normandy yet."

Roosevelt took a long breath.

"It's working," Eisenhower said, his voice barely audible.

Roosevelt nodded, but didn't smile.

"Still," he said, "I keep thinking about that line in Henry V. 'We few, we happy few...'" He shook his head. "How easy it is to speak of honor, when you're not the one storming the beach."

Hopkins offered no response.

After a moment, the President turned to Eisenhower. "You're still convinced Montgomery's the right man to lead the real invasion?"

"He's meticulous. Conservative. Not a gambler. That's exactly what we need."

Roosevelt didn't argue. Instead, he moved to the window and looked out into the sodden night.

"Let's pray Berlin sees only what we want them to see," he said.

"And nothing more," Eisenhower added.

Chapter 10

The Desert Fox in the Fog

★★★ La Roche-Guyon, France – May 1944. Field Marshal Erwin Rommel stood on the parapet of the château's upper terrace, the morning fog drifting across the Seine like breath on glass. Below, in the courtyard, staff officers moved briskly—orders exchanged, maps unrolled, telephones ringing from field desks set up beside sandbags. Trucks unloaded fuel drums beneath the canopy of horse chestnut trees.

France looked peaceful from a distance, but Rommel knew better. He had fought too long, and seen too much, to mistake stillness for safety.

A courier approached with a sheaf of decoded intercepts and field reports. Rommel waved him off. His eyes were fixed across the river valley, where the mist seemed to thicken unnaturally.

"Fog," he murmured. "Always the fog before something breaks."

Behind him, General Hans Speidel stepped out onto the terrace. "Interrogation reports confirm what the Abwehr picked up last week—massive build-up in southeastern England. Troop movements. Radio traffic. Supply trains headed toward Dover."

Rommel remained still. "They want us to believe Calais."

Speidel paused. "You don't?"

"I don't know yet," Rommel admitted. "It's the problem with lies. If they're built well enough, even the truth starts to sound absurd."

He turned from the rail, walking slowly toward the folding table where fresh reconnaissance photographs were spread in neat rows. Dover. Folkestone. The southeastern coast of England. Rows of armor, artillery positions, endless vehicle columns. Yet something about the images unsettled him. The formations looked almost too visible.

Too perfect.

"Hitler believes Calais," Speidel said. "He's moved two divisions north already."

Rommel nodded absently. "And Rundstedt believes in delay. He wants to wait until the first Allied boots hit sand before counterattacking. That's suicide."

"You think they'll land at Normandy?"

"I think," Rommel said, picking up a photograph, "that if I were Eisenhower, I would land where the defenses are weakest, not where the enemy expects me."

Speidel looked at the map. "So what do we do?"

"We prepare for both."

Rommel dropped the photo back onto the table.

"Move the 21st Panzer Division closer to Caen," he ordered. "And strengthen anti-aircraft coverage along the Cotentin. Quietly."

Speidel hesitated. "That may be seen as doubting the Führer's judgment."

Rommel fixed him with a look that belonged more to Africa than Europe. Hard. Sun-forged. Unforgiving.

"I'm not interested in politics," he said. "I'm interested in survival."

Speidel gave a tight nod and withdrew.

Rommel turned back toward the fog. He hated this war now—not for its bloodshed, but for its illusions. In Africa, you saw your enemy. You smelled his oil fires. You heard the engines before the dust rose. But this… this was a war of shadows. Of whispers in diplomatic channels. Of possible phantom armies and unseen couriers.

The English were master illusionists. He admired them for it.

But admiration didn't equal trust. And trust didn't equal readiness.

His thoughts returned to Calais.

Too convenient. Too visible. Too loud.

He stepped back inside the château, where a radio hummed low on the sideboard. He adjusted the dial and paused at a frequency carrying BBC London—barely intelligible but still audible.

A clipped British voice recited the shipping forecast. The words passed over him like smoke.

"Dogger. German Bight. Moderate to poor visibility. Wind south-southeast. Force five…"

Rommel listened not for weather, but for rhythm. For code.

Then came something odd.

A phrase, buried in the report: "The dice are on the carpet."

He froze.

That line had surfaced before. In April, and again last week.

He turned down the volume and moved to his desk. Pulled open a drawer. Inside, a red folder labeled Rösselsprung—Knight's Move. A file on Allied deception operations. Inside: psychological warfare notes, intercepted British broadcasts, codenames, frequencies. Doodles of phrases repeated like prayers.

The dice are on the carpet. The king's breath is glass. The tulip bends at dusk.

Poetry again. And poetry, Rommel had learned, meant preparation.

The war was about to begin.

But where?

That remained the only question that mattered.

He lit a cigarette with steady fingers, smoke curling upward like mist.

If the Allies were coming, let them come. He would not meet them in the fog. He would bring fire.

Chapter 11

Sainte-Mère-Église

★★★ The Norman sky hung heavy and unforgiving—a damp shroud stitched with ragged clouds racing on a biting wind. At exactly 0015 hours on June 6, 1944, the first waves of paratroopers began to spill from the darkened skies over the Cotentin Peninsula. Below, the centuries-old town of Sainte-Mère-Église lay quiet beneath slanted rooftops and slate chimneys—blissfully unaware that history was descending upon it in white silk and fire.

Among the scattered formations descending through the darkness was First Lieutenant Richard Winters of Easy Company, 506th Parachute Infantry Regiment. The jump had gone wrong almost immediately—flak bursting across the sky, formations breaking apart, men dropping miles from their intended zones. Winters hit the ground hard in unfamiliar terrain, alone at first, the silence around him broken only by distant gunfire and the rustle of hedgerows in the wind. He paused only long enough to orient himself, then moved with purpose, gathering what men he could, organizing them quickly—no hesitation, no wasted motion—before pushing toward the sound of the fight.

High above, dozens of C-47 Skytrains droned through the night like an approaching storm. Inside their trembling fuselages, young men sat shoulder-to-shoulder, tethered to steel and faith. Some clutched crucifixes or faded photographs; others gripped rifles with knuckles white. Many held letters, worn soft from anxious hands—a last tether to lives paused thousands of miles across the Atlantic.

Private Ray Collins of the 505th Parachute Infantry Regiment sat rigid, boots hovering an inch above the metal floor—a fleeting weightlessness that felt too much like falling. Silence hung thick between the men. Faces carved from shadow, drained of youth. They were already halfway ghosts.

Across from him, Private Sal Mancini mouthed a whispered prayer, rubbing a tarnished silver dollar between thumb and forefinger. Collins had never been religious, but tonight he wished for something to believe in.

"Stand up! Hook up!" the jumpmaster barked.

Collins rose, heart pounding but hands steady. He clipped his static line with practiced precision. The door slid open. The wind roared in like an angry god. Below, Normandy lay cloaked in darkness, its hedgerows hiding rifle barrels and fate.

The red light flipped to green.

"Go! Go! Go!"

He leapt.

Cold slapped him raw. Air tore past like the first breath of chaos. His chute snapped open, yanking him upward before settling into a slow, shuddering drift toward earth. Far below, the world fractured—orange flickers of fire, tracer rounds clawing skyward.

Sainte-Mère-Église burned faintly in the distance, a farmhouse blaze flickering from earlier in the evening. Villagers fought with buckets; German patrols with rifles. The town teetered on the edge between ordinary life and war's machinery.

Collins twisted in his harness, steering as canopies bloomed like ghostly flowers in the wind. Some drifted peacefully toward the outskirts; others veered off, snagging rooftops and treetops.

"Scheiße! Fallschirmjäger!" a German voice shouted below.

Gunfire erupted. Tracers stitched the sky in red arcs. One parachutist slammed into the church steeple, lines tangling in the spire. He dangled helpless—a grim effigy of invasion.

Another trooper hit the ground hard in the square, cut down before he could free himself.

Collins hit the earth behind a crumbling stone wall. His leg flared but held. He yanked off his chute, gripped his M1, crouched low. Chaos swirled—shouts in English, German, French. Footsteps approached.

A flash: two short, one long. Friendly.

He darted through darkness.

By 0200 hours, the drop had splintered units across the countryside. Men gathered in scattered knots, some ten miles off course. Fog, flak, and faulty navigation unraveled the plan. Maps were useless among the hedgerows. Compass needles wobbled. Passwords whispered like spells.

By the time scattered units began to form into small fighting elements, Winters had assembled only a handful of paratroopers—far fewer than the strength of Easy Company. The invasion, though still unfolding, already bore the marks of disorder. Radios were silent or missing, drop zones misaligned, and no clear sense of the broader battle could be confirmed. Still, the mission held: move, engage, disrupt. Survive.

Still, the objective held: seize Sainte-Mère-Église and the vital crossroads nearby. Without those junctions, German reinforcements could thunder into Utah Beach by sunrise.

Lieutenant James "Jimmy" Colton, lean and steel-eyed from North Africa's deserts, crouched near a hedgerow north of town. Around him, thirty troopers braced in the cold silence.

"We hit 'em fast, hard, from the orchard," he whispered. "They won't expect us behind."

No questions. Eyes met his. Leadership wasn't rank—it was gravity.

They moved. Apple trees cloaked them, leaves slick with dew and ash. Near the square's edge, Colton spotted a faint orange glow—a German cigarette. An MG-34 team waited just ahead.

He signaled. Two men crept forward. The first shot missed; the second found its mark. German fire snapped back. Two Americans fell.

Colton launched a rifle grenade. The orchard exploded in dirt, shouts, and flying bark. They charged—bayonets bared, boots pounding cobblestones.

The square ignited with brutal close-quarter combat. Screams folded into smoke. Faces blurred until you spotted a weapon. Then instinct took over—aim, fire, move.

Inside the church, civilians huddled beneath vaulted naves. Stained glass trembled with every distant blast. A priest whispered Latin prayers. A boy clung to his robes. Outside, the war closed in.

By 0430, Sainte-Mère-Église was under American control—barely. The crossroads secured, but snipers lingered at the edges. Every creak of a door could mean the next bullet.

Barns became makeshift hospitals. Medics worked in bloodied sleeves and near silence. Collins leaned against a stone wall, arm bandaged from a grazing wound, eyes fixed on the church steeple.

A chaplain had climbed to reach the hanging paratrooper—Private John Steele. Incredibly, he was still alive.

"Hell of a way to make an entrance," Collins muttered, voice rough.

Mancini dropped beside him, soot-streaked, wild-eyed. "You think we're still in Normandy?"

Collins gave a thin smile. "I think we just kicked in the front door."

All around, parachutes clung to trees and fields—some empty, some hiding crates, some cloaking the dead. Every canopy told a story: of arrival, courage, sacrifice.

And still, the rumble of armor approached. Not all of it friendly.

Sainte-Mère-Église would become the first French town liberated on D-Day. But in these gray hours before dawn, there was no celebration—only exhaustion, quiet grief, and the shared understanding that the fight ahead would be longer, bloodier, and more defining than anything yet.

They had dropped into darkness. Now they would fight their way into the light.

War does not begin when the first shot is fired.
It begins long before—in the quiet certainty that it must.

Chapter 12

The Field Marshal at Midnight

★★★ Herrlingen, Germany – June 6, 1944. Rain tapped softly against the windows of the Rommel residence as Field Marshal Erwin Rommel sat at the dining table beside his wife, Lucie. The evening had been quiet by wartime standards—muted conversation, candlelight softened by the storm outside, and the rare illusion that Europe had paused long enough to breathe.

It was Lucie's birthday.

For the first time in weeks, Rommel allowed himself a moment away from maps and concrete bunkers, from endless inspections along the Atlantic Wall and arguments with Berlin over armor deployment. The weather over the Channel had deteriorated badly through the night and into the morning—high winds, rough seas, low clouds. Conditions no sane commander would choose for invasion.

Rommel had trusted the weather.

That trust lasted until the telephone rang.

The sound cut through the house like artillery.

Rommel rose immediately. Years of war had conditioned him to recognize urgency before a word was spoken. By the time he reached the receiver, the operator was already connecting Paris command.

"Field Marshal," came the strained voice on the line, "reports are arriving from Normandy. Airborne landings near Sainte-Mère-

Église. Naval bombardments along the coast. Multiple sectors engaged."

Rommel's expression hardened instantly.

"How large?"

"We don't yet know."

Another voice entered the line—fainter, hurried. Conflicting reports. Paratroopers scattered inland. Radar confusion. Coastal batteries under fire. Communications failing.

Rommel stared toward the rain-darkened window.

For several seconds he said nothing.

Then quietly:

"So, they came through the storm."

Lucie stood silently in the doorway, watching him. She understood immediately. The war had returned to claim him again.

Within minutes, Rommel was dressed in field gray, aides scrambling through the residence gathering maps, dispatch cases, and coded documents. Staff cars waited outside beneath cold rain and headlamps. The roads south toward France were already crowded with military traffic and confusion.

As the convoy pushed through the darkness toward La Roche-Guyon, reports continued arriving in fragments.

Normandy.

Multiple landings reported along the Normandy coastline. Airborne troops scattered inland. Communications from several coastal sectors already failing.

Was this the invasion?

Or merely the diversion before Calais?

That question hung over every headquarters in occupied France.

Even now, Hitler's command structure hesitated. Some believed Normandy was only a feint designed to pull German reserves away from Pas-de-Calais before Patton's "real" invasion force crossed farther north.

Rommel feared the hesitation more than the landings themselves.

The convoy crossed into France beneath low clouds and intermittent rain. Dawn faded into gray afternoon, then evening. Burned-out vehicles lined portions of the road. Luftwaffe aircraft roared overhead sporadically, chased at times by Allied fighters that now seemed to own the skies.

By the time Rommel arrived back at La Roche-Guyon late on June 6, exhaustion and urgency had settled over the château like smoke.

The headquarters no longer resembled the composed command center he had left behind days earlier.

Telephones rang continuously. Officers moved between map tables carrying casualty figures and fragmented field reports. Orderlies rushed through corridors clutching dispatch folders still damp from transport. "The entire building vibrated with the nervous energy of men struggling to keep pace with events already overtaking them."

General Hans Speidel met Rommel immediately near the operations room.

"The Americans have secured positions west of the Vire," Speidel said quickly. "British and Canadian forces are pressing inland near Caen. Airborne units are disrupting road movement throughout the Cotentin."

Rommel removed his gloves slowly, eyes fixed on the massive operations map spread across the table.

"And Calais?" he asked.

Speidel hesitated.

"No major movement yet."

That answer disturbed Rommel more than if Calais had erupted entirely.

He leaned over the map, tracing the Normandy coastline with two fingers while officers nearby continued arguing over reserve deployment and Panzer authorization. Every delay now carried consequences measured in beaches, roads, and blood.

"The Allies want confusion," Rommel said quietly. "And we are giving it to them."

He straightened and looked around the room.

For months he had warned Berlin that the invasion must be crushed at the shoreline. Once the Allies established a foothold inland, Germany's shrinking ability to maneuver armor beneath Allied air superiority would become catastrophic.

Rommel stood alone in the study, his tall figure framed by the flickering light of a kerosene lamp. The greatcoat hung heavy on his shoulders, collar turned up against the draft sneaking through the ancient mortar. His presence filled the room—not with bluster, but with a quiet, fierce intensity. He looked less like the celebrated "Desert Fox" of newspapers and more like a man trying to hold back a storm with his bare hands.

On the oak table before him, dispatches, teletypes, and coded transmissions lay scattered beneath a grease-smeared map of the Normandy coast. Red grease-pencil circles marked Vierville-sur-Mer, Colleville, Sainte-Mère-Église, and the Orne bridges. Intercepted reports from the 91st and 716th Infantry Divisions confirmed the worst: Allied paratroopers had landed in force. Scattered reports indicated American paratroopers operating in fragmented groups, some units cut off entirely from their original commands. Landing craft approached beaches west of Bayeux. German positions were already being overrun.

Rommel leaned closer, gloved hand steady as he tapped a small town south of Bayeux.

There.

The pivot point. The fulcrum.

If the Allies seized the Caen-Bayeux corridor and controlled the inland road junctions, they would split the German front, driving a wedge between the 7th Army and the Panzer Lehr Division. If secured before reinforcements arrived, the Wehrmacht would never push them back into the sea.

He turned sharply toward the door and called, voice low but urgent. "Spaetz!"

Major Helmut Spaetz appeared within seconds, boots snapping on flagstone. He looked barely awake, uniform hastily buttoned, eyes wide with dawning realization: the long-dreaded invasion was real.

"Wake General Feuchtinger," Rommel ordered, voice a blade cutting the quiet. "Tell him the 21st Panzer Division must move. Tanks rolling toward Caen by first light."

Spaetz hesitated—not from defiance, but from the weight of military bureaucracy. "Mein Feldmarschall… orders from Oberkommando der Wehrmacht require Führer's direct authorization for Panzergruppe movement. It must come from Hitler himself."

Rommel's gaze froze on Spaetz—cold, precise, unyielding. He had already run the calculus of disaster in his mind countless times. There was no time for politics.

"If we wait for Berlin, Caen will fall," Rommel said evenly. "If Caen falls, they have the Orne. And if they hold the Orne, they drive straight into the heart of France. We will not stop them with bicycles and rifles."

Spaetz swallowed hard, then nodded. "Jawohl."

"Go," Rommel said, returning to the map. "Tell Feuchtinger I'm assuming direct operational control. Let Berlin challenge me later, if they dare."

Spaetz vanished down the hall, boots echoing away.

Rommel exhaled slowly, placing both hands on the table. The room was silent again—save for the ticking clock and the distant thunder that no longer seemed distant at all. He stared down the mess of papers, foggy reports, and the staggering truth inked in blood. Eisenhower had done it. The Allies had landed in Normandy, not Pas-de-Calais. The entire German defense had been baited.

Patton's phantom First U.S. Army Group—FUSAG—had been a masterpiece of deception. Radio chatter, dummy tanks, inflatable aircraft, double agents—Berlin had swallowed it whole. Even now, Hitler's staff clung to the illusion that Normandy was a feint.

Fools, Rommel thought bitterly.

Eisenhower had gambled everything on the sector the High Command had left most vulnerable—not desperation, but genius.

He opened the window. The latch creaked as cold air rolled in, slicing through the lamp's warmth. Somewhere above the clouds, the drone of C-47s continued—more paratroopers, more supplies, relentless precision. Below, Normandy's fields lay drenched in moonlight and anticipation. Villages slept under the weight of coming violence.

Rommel lingered at the window, breathing the night air as though it might carry the scent of what was to come. He was no mystic, but decades of campaigns had taught him how to recognize when history shifted beneath your feet. Tonight, it had.

His thoughts drifted to Manfred, his barely teenage son. To Lucie, his wife far away in Ulm. And deeper still, to the oath he had taken—not merely to Hitler, but to defend Germany. What had the Führer done? Hoarded power, micromanaged field commanders, delayed crucial armor moves out of fear.

The war had once felt winnable—in North Africa, in early France. Tonight, it felt like reckoning.

He traced the jagged coastline on the map—Vierville-sur-Mer, Colleville, Sainte-Mère-Église, the beaches stretching east toward Bayeux. Beneath each name, the grim potential of collapse.

With quiet determination, he drew a line inland from the beaches, following roads through Carentan and Saint-Lô. The pencil scraped its way toward Paris.

That was the endgame. Whether Berlin saw it or not.

"Not this time," he whispered.

Rommel lifted the field telephone receiver. His voice, when he spoke, was steel.

"This is Field Marshal Rommel. I am issuing direct operational orders to the 21st Panzer Division and all mobile units within range of Caen. Execute countermeasures immediately. I will take full responsibility."

What he was doing skirted the edge of insubordination. In Berlin, that line was not just dangerous—it was fatal. But the clock was ticking. Waiting for permission would mean losing the war before sunrise.

He wasn't gambling for Hitler's approval. He was gambling for France.

Outside, the eastern sky brightened faintly. Birds had yet to sing. But the war was fully awake.

Rommel stood in the half-light of his study, jacketed in the weight of command, eyes fixed on the battlefield beyond.

History was coming for them all.

And Erwin Rommel—soldier, patriot, reluctant rebel—would not meet it asleep.

Chapter 13

The Lost Cause

★★★ June 6, 1944. The dawn never came. A slate curtain of cloud smothered the Normandy coast, blurring sea and sky into a single indistinct plane. Waves heaved beneath landing craft that pitched and groaned like iron beasts pushed toward slaughter. Overhead, thunder rolled—not from weather, but from flak bursts rending the air around darkened transport planes. Operation Overlord had begun. Months of preparation. Years of anticipation. And already, it was unraveling.

In the morning darkness before first light, American paratroopers of the 82nd and 101st Airborne Divisions dropped into the Norman countryside. But the carefully plotted landing zones dissolved into fog and chaos. British gliders released too soon. Parachutes yanked open over flooded fields. Many troops plunged into icy water behind Utah Beach—drowned by their own equipment in bogs seeded with wire traps and wooden stakes. Radios sputtered or failed. Squads disappeared into the terrain, unaccounted for and unreachable. Some regrouped. Most never reached their targets.

Lieutenant Winters and the remnants of his improvised group moved cautiously through the bocage, advancing by instinct more than direction. What had begun as a coordinated airborne assault had devolved into isolated pockets of resistance. The larger plan was no longer visible—only the immediate objective of survival and movement remained.

Under orders relayed through fragmented channels, surviving elements began moving west toward the coastline in small, scattered groups. Winters led a handful of men through hedgerows and narrow lanes under constant threat of German patrols. The movement was slow, disjointed, and often blind. By the time they reached the outer approaches to the beach, the full scale of the withdrawal was evident—landing craft pulling away under fire, the shoreline choked with the remnants of a failed operation.

On higher ground, troopers who made landfall intact were scattered, often miles from their designated drop points. Maps became meaningless in the twisted lanes and hedgerows of bocage country. Compass needles swung erratically. Crossroads remained in enemy hands. Bridges stayed unblown. The airborne assault, intended to fracture German reinforcement routes, dissolved into misfires and isolation.

By late morning, the realization began to take hold. The invasion was not consolidating—it was unraveling. The anticipated linkup with amphibious forces had not materialized. German resistance was strengthening, not collapsing. Winters understood then what few were willing to say aloud: they were no longer supporting an invasion—they were cut off behind enemy lines.

And then the sea turned against them.

Crosscurrents drove entire waves of landing craft off course. At Omaha Beach—deemed difficult but necessary—American infantry landed behind schedule, out of position, and with no effective naval or aerial cover. The First Infantry Division was meant to storm ashore behind a shield of smoke and shelling. But the bombardment missed its targets. German bunkers, reinforced in secret, emerged untouched. Fire zones overlapped like a spider's web. German MG-42 machine gun crews fired without pause.

When the ramps dropped, the surf turned red.

Sherman DD tanks—twenty-nine in total—were released too far offshore. Tossed in swells and hampered by design flaws, most sank before reaching sand. Only two crawled ashore. The infantry followed without armor, stumbling through surf under a storm of steel. Many never made it past the waterline. Captain Leonard Meyers of the 116th Regiment was struck three times in the chest before he could shout an order. Medics attempting to reach him died in his wake.

Aboard the USS Augusta, General Omar Bradley stared through binoculars at the carnage on Omaha. The air between ship and shore shimmered with smoke and shock. "They're not moving," he said, more to himself than anyone else.

His aide nodded grimly. "Sir, it's a massacre."

Wave after wave arrived with no clear path forward. Communication collapsed. Company lines tangled. Troops crouched behind Czech hedgehogs and the dead, unable to advance, unwilling to retreat. Mortars rained from the cliffs. German gunners—well-fed, well-armed, and untouched by bombardment—had no reason to stop firing.

Behind the lines, Lieutenant James "Jimmy" Colton crouched near a hedgerow, thirty men at his side. The orchard surrounding Sainte-Mère-Église was quiet for the moment, dew glistening on apple leaves and rifle barrels. They had dropped ten miles off course. Fog, flak, and wind had done their work.

Still, the objective stood: take the town, hold the crossroads. Otherwise, German armor would reach Utah Beach before the tide could carry the wounded back.

"We hit 'em from the orchard," Colton whispered. "Fast, hard. They won't expect that."

His men nodded. No questions. Their belief rested in his voice, not his rank.

They moved.

A cigarette glow marked the enemy position. The first shot missed. The second found bone. A German MG 34 raked the orchard. Two Americans dropped. Colton's grenade shattered the calm—then came boots on cobblestones, bayonets, shouts.

Inside the church, civilians clung to one another beneath stained glass windows that rattled with every blast. A priest whispered Latin. A child whimpered.

By 0430, the town was tenuously under American control. But snipers remained. The church bell had stopped tolling, but not the war.

Smoke drifted through the square in gray ribbons as scattered rifle fire cracked somewhere beyond the stone buildings. Burning parachutes hung from trees like torn ghosts. One of the transport planes still smoldered in a distant pasture, its twisted fuselage casting a dull orange glow against the hedgerows.

Near the church steps, Corporal Mancini crouched beside Collins, whose sleeve was soaked dark with blood.

"You think we're where we're supposed to be?" Mancini asked quietly.

Collins looked toward the steeple, where Private John Steele still hung suspended against the church tower, barely moving in the cold wind.

"I think," Collins muttered, breathing hard, "we're wherever the war decided to drop us."

All around them, the carefully plotted invasion had dissolved into fragments.

American paratroopers from the 82nd and 101st Airborne Divisions fought in isolated pockets across the Norman countryside, many miles from their intended objectives. British gliders had landed scattered across flooded fields and hedgerows, some releasing too early in darkness and fog. Units that were supposed to move with precision now searched desperately for officers, radios, maps, or simply familiar faces.

No one possessed a clear picture of the battlefield anymore.

German MG-42 machine gun crews fired without pause from concealed positions overlooking narrow roads and village crossings. Every hedgerow seemed capable of hiding a rifleman. Even farmhouse windows became potential firing points.

The invasion had begun.

But already, it was slipping beyond the control of the men who had planned it.

In the distance, artillery rolled across the Norman countryside with a low, endless thunder. The horizon pulsed faintly with naval bombardment from the Channel beyond the unseen hills.

Collins adjusted his helmet and slowly rose to one knee.

"What now?" Mancini asked.

Collins checked the last magazine in his rifle.

"Now," he said grimly, "we find out how much of the invasion survived the landing."

Behind them, the church tower loomed over Sainte-Mère-Église like a dark monument rising through smoke and drifting ash.

And across Normandy, thousands of Allied soldiers were beginning to realize the same terrible truth:

The battle for France was not unfolding according to plan.

Speed changes war.
Understanding it wins it.

Chapter 14

The President's Advisor

★★★ June 13, 1944. Admiral William D. Leahy stood alone by the arched window of his West Wing office, eyes tracing the morning haze clinging to the White House lawn like battlefield smoke. In his hand, a worn manila folder bulged with newspaper clippings, internal memos, and confidential reports. All focused on one man: General George S. Patton.

Leahy had seen war from every angle—at sea, in council rooms—but now he navigated a new front: the perilous space between military urgency and political survival. As Chief of Staff to the Commander-in-Chief, he was Roosevelt's most trusted military confidant, a steady keel amid America's war machine striking a reef.

June 6 had gone terribly wrong. The second front—long promised—was blood-soaked failure. Landing craft torn to splinters by German guns. Airborne divisions scattered or drowned in flooded marshes. Normandy's beaches, once envisioned as the crucible of liberation, had become a graveyard of ambition.

The president's internal polling—still favoring reelection—showed slow erosion of public faith. The nation was exhausted. Victory promised; sacrifice delivered. And in London, Churchill faced his own reckoning.

Leahy turned from the window, exhaling slowly. The folder—Patton's glories, scandals, and unfiltered remarks—weighed heavier than paper. Could this blunt, brash man become the salvation of the Western Front?

The next morning, sunlight filtered softly through gauzy curtains in Roosevelt's private study. The president sat propped in bed, a silver tray across his lap. A Berliner Pfannkuchen—his favored jelly-filled German donut—rested beside steaming coffee. The room held the hush of responsibility, broken only by the tick of the mantel clock and rustle of morning papers.

Leahy was among the few permitted into this sanctuary.

Roosevelt looked up as the admiral entered, smile faint and worn.

"Bill," he said, gesturing him forward, "have a donut. They're fresh. I'd offer a cigarette, but I know you won't touch the things."

Leahy remained standing, folder under arm.

"Thank you, Mr. President. I've had my fill this morning—of both donuts and difficult decisions."

Roosevelt raised an eyebrow, amusement flickering.

"That's an ominous opening, even for you. Sit."

Leahy eased into the chair beside the bed and laid the folder across his knees.

"Sir, we need to talk about the next move in Europe."

Roosevelt exhaled.

"I've been dreading that conversation. Marshall wants options. Eisenhower looks hollow. The British are rattled, and Congress is sharpening its knives. What are you thinking?"

Leahy opened the folder, revealing a black-and-white photograph of Patton in steel helmet, ivory-handled revolvers at his hips, chin thrust forward like a man trying to will the war into retreat.

"I believe," Leahy said slowly, "it's time to give the bastard another shot."

Roosevelt's head tilted back. Humor drained.

"Patton?"

"Yes, sir."

"You're serious."

"I am."

A long pause. Roosevelt sipped his coffee deliberately.

"You've spent two years lecturing me about that man's lack of restraint. Now you want to hand him another army?"

Leahy leaned forward.

"I've spent two years watching every commander in this war. Patton has flaws—hell, he is a flaw in many ways—but he's also the most aggressive, instinctual field commander we have. The Germans fear him. They respect him. They believe he's the tip of our spear—and after Normandy, we need to make that belief real."

Roosevelt tapped a finger against the donut, seeking clarity.

"You think he can recover from the Italian incident?"

Leahy nodded.

"The slapping scandal did damage—but it didn't break him. Eisenhower used him brilliantly as a decoy in Operation Fortitude. The Germans were convinced he'd lead the invasion. That bought us time. That's leverage. Let's use it."

The president set down his coffee.

"Bill, every advisor I have—Marshall, King, even Ike himself—will raise hell over this."

"I know. And I'll face them," Leahy said.

"But ask yourself: who else can organize a second assault, on short notice, and turn it into victory? Who else has the force of will to punch through German defenses before they harden?"

Roosevelt looked down at the folder's pages. Reports, headlines, memos—a story unfinished.

"The British will have a fit."

"They'll recover. Montgomery's pride will smart, and Churchill will need convincing. But Churchill wants a win almost as badly as we do. Deep down, he knows Patton might be the only man who can deliver."

Roosevelt's eyes met his.

"And what if Patton blunders again? What if this becomes another humiliation?"

Leahy hesitated for a moment.

"Then we'll own it. But if we delay, the Germans entrench. And the Soviets? They'll take Eastern Europe city by city—and they won't leave. If we don't move now, we may win the war—but lose the peace."

The president leaned back, weariness settling deep. He looked out the window, where morning sunlight cast long shadows across a quiet, wounded capital.

"I called you my 'leg man' to the press," he murmured. "Meant it as a compliment. You digest the impossible and make it palatable."

He paused.

"I'm flying to London in two days. The summit with Churchill will proceed. Let's blindside him with this."

"Yes, Mr. President."

"Brief the Joint Chiefs. Gauge their temperature. Prepare a full proposal for Eisenhower and Marshall. We'll need a careful roll-out—God help us, a political one."

"I'll see it done."

"And if you get pushback?"

Roosevelt's eyes locked with his.

"Then remind them this war will not be won by comfort, consensus, or caution. It will be won by conviction. Yours, mine—and God help us—maybe even Patton's."

Leahy rose, hesitated at the door.

"Sir, if we don't move fast—if we let the Soviets carry the burden alone—Eastern Europe will be theirs before we reach the Rhine."

Roosevelt's face turned grave.

"I know. And when they raise their flag over Warsaw or Prague, they won't lower it again."

He glanced at Lincoln's portrait across the room.

"We may have lost a battle, Bill. But we cannot lose the balance of a continent."

Outside the White House windows, dawn spilled light across a city bracing for harder days.

Leahy saluted crisply and turned to go. Just as the door clicked shut behind him, Roosevelt called after him.

"Bill."

"Yes, sir?"

"If this works—if—you'll be the one who lit the fire. Just make sure it doesn't burn us all down."

Leahy allowed himself the faintest smile.

"Understood, sir."

Outside, in the hall, he paused, turning back toward the window where the summer sun touched the lawn with soft gold, masking the raw edge beneath. The next battle would not be fought with bullets or bombs—but with persuasion, risk, and raw determination.

And perhaps—just perhaps—with Patton at the helm, the tide might turn.

A commander is measured not by his orders—
but by how men move when he is silent.

Chapter 15

Summoned and Supplanted

★★★ June 16, 1944. Just after midnight, a courier arrived at Greenham Lodge, a damp, ivy-clad estate deep in the Berkshire countryside—far from the command chatter of Portsmouth and London's war rooms. Once a modest noble seat, it had become a gilded cage.

General George S. Patton had spent six long weeks here, a lion in ceremonial exile. Officially "assigned to strategic deception operations" under SHAEF, in truth he had become a ghost—paraded for aerial reconnaissance, photographed beside papier-mâché tanks, wielded as a boogeyman to scare the Germans into guarding Calais.

They feared him.

But he led nothing.

Not yet.

He sat in a worn leather armchair by the hearth, a heavy wool blanket around his legs, thumbing through *On War* by Clausewitz—again—when the knock echoed through the manor's paneled halls.

Colonel Charles Codman entered, hat in hand, followed by a young signals officer carrying a sealed envelope. The courier offered it without a word.

"From General Marshall's office, sir," the young man said. "Marked Priority Ultra."

Patton's finger stiffened as he broke the wax seal. He read the message once. He read it once more, slower now.

TO: GENERAL GEORGE S. PATTON, UNITED STATES ARMY
BY: DIRECT ORDER OF THE CHIEF OF STAFF.
YOU ARE TO REPORT IMMEDIATELY TO WASHINGTON, D.C.
PRIORITY AIR TRANSPORT ARRANGED OUT OF RAF GREENHAM COMMON. YOU WILL RECEIVE FURTHER INSTRUCTION UPON ARRIVAL.
SIGNED: GEORGE C. MARSHALL

He stared at the words as if they might shift beneath his gaze. "Charlie," he said slowly, not looking up, "have I done something again?"

Codman blinked. "Sir?"

"Something… unforgivable. Slapped the wrong man. Insulted the wrong people. Offended a bishop. Something they've only now decided to court-martial me over."

Codman fought a smile. "If you did, sir, I somehow missed it."

Patton rose, boots thudding softly on wood as he paced. "Washington doesn't summon a sidelined general out of nowhere unless they want to pin a medal or dig a grave. I'm not due a medal."

He paused by the frost-streaked window, peering into the fog-draped garden. The scent of chimney smoke and wet ivy drifted in with the breeze.

"They buried me once. Are they digging me up—or burying me deeper?"

The C-47 Skytrain groaned through upper altitudes—cold, stripped bare inside. Patton sat alone, belted into a canvas seat, thick flight jacket cinched tight. His ivory-handled revolver gleamed beneath his coat. He hadn't worn it in weeks. Tonight, it felt right again.

The crew left him to his silence.

His thoughts were louder than engines. What did Marshall want? Eisenhower's doing? A power play? A trap? Or—God help them all—a second chance?

He thought of Sicily. The jeers. The scandals. The editorials and whispers in command halls. He had taken it—gritted his teeth, played the ghost.

But Normandy had failed.

And now they call me?

Across the Channel, under a gray morning sky in Portsmouth, Field Marshal Bernard Law Montgomery stood in headquarters, arms crossed behind his back as he read a telegram from the War Cabinet.

He read it once. Twice. Then slower.

General George S. Patton shall assume overall command of the forthcoming Allied assault on the western coast of France.

Montgomery laid the paper down with mechanical care, aligning corners precisely. His face did not change. Stillness absolute—marble awaiting the sculptor's blow.

A knock at the tent flap.

"Enter," he said without turning.

Major General Freddie de Guingand stepped in. "Sir, Downing Street is on the secure line. The Prime Minister wishes to speak with you directly."

Montgomery exhaled faintly. "Of course he does."

The line crackled as he lifted the receiver.

"Bernard," Churchill began, gravelly over wire. "I trust you've read the communiqué."

"I have." His tone was clipped steel.

"I won't dress this in lace," Churchill said. "You and I both know why Normandy failed. Too careful. Too slow. Patton will not make that mistake."

"With respect, Prime Minister," Montgomery said, each syllable chiseled, "Patton is no strategist. He's a butcher. Charges first, draws the map afterward."

"True," Churchill said. "But he moves. And right now, Bernard, movement is what we need. Europe watches. So does Moscow. Roosevelt and I agree—there's no one else."

Montgomery's knuckles whitened against the receiver.

"Will I retain command of British ground forces?"

"You will coordinate with Patton," Churchill replied. Then, after a pause: "But he will have final say on operational tempo. The Americans won't accept another Overlord without one of their own in command. And the Soviets won't accept another delay."

Montgomery was silent.

"I know it stings," Churchill softened. "But think of the men. Think of the war. Patton's recklessness may be the fuel we need. Precision has not served us. Perhaps fury will."

Montgomery closed his eyes briefly. "Understood."

He replaced the receiver without another word.

Montgomery lowered the binoculars slowly, his expression unreadable.

Somewhere out there, across the waters, a man he despised had just been lifted from the grave and hurled into the center of the war.

Montgomery exhaled.

"So be it," he muttered. "Let the barbarian have his war."

Chapter 16

Echoes of a Hollow Victory

★★★ Berlin had not known true joy in years. What remained was brittle laughter, forced smiles, and a hollow parody of triumph. Yet on this warm June evening in 1944, the heart of the Reich pulsed with a cruel imitation of celebration.

The air above the capital shimmered with false euphoria. Crimson banners hung from soot-streaked balconies, snapping in the breeze like bloodied standards from an older, more honest war. Swastikas flapped over silent courtyards and shuttered windows, their shadows stretching long in the dying sunlight. From the Reich Chancellery to the Unter den Linden boulevard, marching bands played triumphal marches, their brass notes masking the distant thrum of departing trains.

Berlin was ablaze with fireworks and self-deception—a fragile empire dressing its wounds with velvet and schnapps. The Reich celebrated not peace, not victory—but survival. And even that, perhaps, only for a night.

Inside the marble halls of government, beneath crystal chandeliers and eagle-carved columns, a banquet unfolded in grotesque splendor. Long linen-draped tables groaned beneath silver trays of roast game, towers of sugared fruit, and champagne flutes flickering like fragile jewels. Generals and ministers clustered in tight, smiling knots. The scent of smoke and perfume mingled with stewed venison and slow-fading fear.

Generalfeldmarschall Wilhelm Keitel lifted his glass with clipped precision. Heinz Guderian chuckled at a joke from Speer. Even the normally reptilian Admiral Dönitz managed a sly grin. Laughter rose like steam.

And at the heart of it all sat Erwin Rommel—back from the front, the supposed architect of salvation, the man whose name was now being whispered as Germany's last true general.

His feldgrau uniform was immaculate. His Knight's Cross gleamed against his collar. He sat erect, his expression schooled in stoicism. To anyone watching, he looked the part: composed, contained, respected.

But his hands remained still.

And his gaze was elsewhere.

He despised these gatherings.

Toasts made over bleeding maps. Medals pinned while boys screamed in bombed-out trenches. A thousand glasses lifted to illusory gains while coffins stacked in hospital corridors. He had seen real victory—quick, clean, earned. This was theater. Theater for a nation bleeding from the inside out.

Beside him, Lucia Maria Rommel rested a hand lightly over his. Her dark blue gown shimmered under the chandeliers. Her silver edelweiss brooch, subtle and Alpine, drew more attention than she did. She smiled when appropriate. Nodded when expected. But beneath the veneer, her eyes searched his face.

"You're far away," she said softly, bending close.

Rommel forced a smile. "Only in thought."

"They say you turned back five divisions with half the fuel and none of the reserves you requested."

"I did what I had to," he replied. Then quieter: "It wasn't enough."

She didn't press further.

Between courses, Rommel stepped away, navigating a side corridor to a small antechamber with tall windows facing the

Wilhelmstrasse. Fireworks burst silently above the rooftops. Beyond them, smoke lingered over the city's eastern districts—real smoke, from the last Allied air raid two nights prior. No one spoke of it now. Celebration had boundaries.

Rommel removed his gloves slowly and studied the map in silence. Then he walked to the window and stood with a cup of black coffee growing cold in his hand. He thought of the men left behind—scattered through French hedgerows, buried under collapsed farmhouses, still gripping rifles long after their breath had faded. He thought of Africa, where victory had been honest and defeat had taught something. France had taught only futility.

Lucia joined him a moment later. For a while, neither spoke.

Then she said, "You were right about the landing zone. They came through Normandy after all."

"I knew they would," he murmured. "But Berlin wouldn't listen. Calais was easier to believe. Easier to defend. And now…"

He didn't finish.

The door creaked behind them. Albert Speer stepped in, wine glass in hand. "Ah, our lion has wandered," he said with a smile too wide.

Rommel turned, expression unreadable. "Just getting some air."

"Come back in. Guderian's telling stories again. He insists you once led a charge from a captured bicycle."

Rommel allowed a humorless grin. "That story improves with every retelling."

Speer leaned in, voice lowered. "They're watching you, Erwin. More than ever now."

Rommel nodded once. "Let them."

Later that night, Rommel returned to his quarters alone. The light from the hallway flickered on and off as he passed. The air carried the faint echo of laughter—detached, joyless. He removed his tunic with mechanical precision, folding it carefully before placing it on the chair by the hearth. Outside, distant artillery—far away, from somewhere beyond the horizon—boomed faintly.

He stood in his undershirt and trousers before the mirror, his reflection less soldier than shadow.

He whispered something only he could hear.

Then he sat at his desk and began to write—not reports, not declarations, but a letter to his son. The words came slowly at first. Then steadily.

He wrote of honor.

Of disillusionment.

Of legacy.

And finally, of peace—earned not in conquest, but in truth.

Chapter 17

Winds of Reckoning

★★★ The polished mahogany table in the Cabinet War Rooms gleamed under the soft lamplight, maps stretched across its surface like wounded terrain. Red pencils, cigarette stubs, and half-drunk cups of tea littered the scene—remnants of frantic discussions carried through days and sleepless nights. The air smelled of musty stone and burnt tobacco—a cavern of quiet defiance deep beneath the blitzed city. London, July 1944.

President Franklin D. Roosevelt had arrived the night before, wearied by the transatlantic flight but sharp as ever in mind. His convoy had been routed through shadowed back streets under cover of night, guarded by British Home Guard and American MPs alike. Now, seated across from Winston Churchill, Roosevelt found himself staring not at a partner in victory, but at a man visibly strained by recent defeat.

Churchill slouched in his chair, a fresh cigar smoldering between his fingers. His eyes were darker than usual, his skin pale beneath the flickering lamplight.

"I won't lie to you, Franklin," he muttered, voice gravelly, "the Commons have been tearing strips from me ever since the Normandy failure. They smell blood in the water. Some want to make the beaches our Gallipoli."

Roosevelt nodded slowly. "I've got no shortage of critics back home either, Winston. One paper in Chicago called it the

'Gettysburg of the Atlantic.' My opponent in the election—what's left of him—is trying to say I've sacrificed boys for a photo op."

Churchill grunted. "That's the price of statesmanship, my friend. But this—this failure—has shaken the empire. We've lost men, lost face, and if we don't act quickly, we may lose the initiative for good."

The underground operations room beneath Whitehall carried the stale heat of sleepless men and overworked machinery. Cigarette smoke from aides and staff officers drifted beneath exposed pipes and low concrete beams, trapped beneath the ceiling like battlefield fog. Maps of Normandy covered the central table, their once-clean invasion arrows now overwritten with casualty estimates, collapsed positions, and uncertain reports arriving by the hour.

Winston Churchill stood near the far end of the chamber beneath the harsh glow of recessed lamps, his cigar resting untouched between two fingers. The heavy folds beneath his eyes revealed the strain of the past several days. Somewhere above the bunker, distant anti-aircraft guns rolled faintly through the London night.

The optimism that had surrounded Operation Overlord only days earlier had evaporated.

Omaha and Utah remained contested killing grounds. British forces at Sword and Gold had advanced only marginally inland before encountering concentrated German resistance. Canadian troops at Juno had suffered catastrophic losses attempting to push beyond the beachhead. Airborne units remained scattered across the Norman countryside, many still isolated and fighting without coherent command structure.

Churchill slowly removed his spectacles and rubbed tired eyes. "The Germans recovered faster than expected," he muttered.

Admiral William D. Leahy sat calmly at the opposite side of the table, posture rigid despite the hour. A half-finished cup of cold coffee rested near his elbow beside a stack of dispatches from Eisenhower's headquarters.

"They recovered because they were never fully broken," Leahy replied evenly.

Churchill looked toward the maps again, jaw tightening.

"And now Washington believes Patton is the answer."

The room fell briefly silent.

The decision had already been made. Patton's reassignment and expanding authority were moving rapidly through Allied command channels, carried forward by desperation as much as confidence.

Churchill exhaled slowly through his nose.

"The Americans place extraordinary faith in him," he said quietly. "Sometimes I wonder whether they mistake aggression for strategy."

Leahy folded his hands together.

"With respect, Prime Minister, aggression may be the only thing preventing a complete collapse of the lodgment."

Churchill turned away from the maps.

"And Montgomery?" he asked. "He knows the terrain. He understands the realities of this campaign. I would prefer to salvage this operation with a man who values caution rather than spectacle."

Leahy's expression barely shifted.

"Montgomery understands caution," he said. "Patton understands recovery."

A faint vibration passed through the concrete floor as another communication relay activated somewhere deeper within the command complex.

Churchill stared down at the invasion maps spread across the table. Red grease-pencil circles marked German armored concentrations moving toward the coast. Several Allied unit markers had already been crossed out entirely.

"He also understands profanity, insubordination, and headlines," Churchill muttered darkly.

For the first time that evening, the corner of Leahy's mouth moved slightly.

"Possibly," he admitted. "But at the moment, sir, the Germans understand momentum."

The words lingered in the stale air.

Churchill said nothing for several seconds. Finally, he placed the untouched cigar beside the map table and looked once more toward Normandy.

"God help us," he said quietly, "if George Patton is truly the only man capable of pulling this invasion back from disaster."

Neither man spoke after that.

Beyond the Channel, thousands of Allied soldiers still fought in darkness, smoke, and shattered hedgerows while the future of the entire Western Front hung in the balance.

***

Patton, newly recalled, stormed into planning rooms like a caged beast. That is, until Eisenhower ordered him to redirect that pent-up energy toward a monumental undertaking: the Normandy Rescue Mission.

The invasion had failed.

Thousands of Allied soldiers remained trapped along isolated stretches of the Norman coastline and countryside, many cut off from organized command and steadily being compressed by tightening German counterattacks. Scattered American, British, and Canadian units now faced annihilation or surrender if extraction could not be organized quickly.

Most Allied commanders viewed a rescue operation as nearly impossible.

Patton did not.

Within days, he assembled a desperate evacuation plan built primarily around Higgins boats, small coastal craft, and hastily reorganized naval coordination teams operating from southern England. The operation depended upon speed, confusion, and deception more than overwhelming force.

German commanders fully expected the Allies to attempt rescue operations near the original invasion sectors. Anticipating such a move, armored units and artillery batteries quietly positioned themselves along likely extraction points, waiting to crush any returning Allied flotilla.

Patton anticipated that expectation.

Under strict secrecy, Allied signal corps operators transmitted carefully manipulated radio traffic suggesting evacuation efforts would occur farther east along a heavily contested section of coastline. German intercept stations received exactly what Patton intended them to hear.

The trap was set.

During the night before the rescue operation, British and Canadian Mosquito fighter-bombers struck the suspected German staging areas with devastating precision. Low-flying aircraft roared across the Norman coast under darkness, strafing concealed armor formations, supply trucks, artillery batteries, and infantry units gathered to ambush the anticipated Allied landing force.

By dawn, fires burned across miles of shattered coastline.

While German forces scrambled to respond to the unexpected air assault, Allied rescue craft moved quietly toward a lesser-defended stretch of beach farther west.

There, beneath smoke, confusion, and the distant rumble of artillery, thousands of exhausted Allied soldiers were pulled from the collapsing lodgment and carried back across the Channel.

Among them was Lieutenant James Colton.

Cold, exhausted, and barely able to stand, he watched the French coastline slowly disappear into gray morning haze as the overloaded Higgins boat carried him away from the disaster that had consumed Normandy.

Behind him, Europe still burned.

Ahead of him, the war was entering a far darker chapter.

Chapter 18

Patton's Second Front

★★★ The tarmac outside the military installation near Washington, D.C., shimmered in the midday heat, the summer air thick as engine oil. Cicadas droned in the trees lining the compound, their relentless hum forming an ambient rhythm beneath the distant thrum of aircraft overhead. The heat wrapped around everything like a damp wool blanket.

General George S. Patton stepped from the olive-drab transport vehicle with the casual sharpness of a man both used to war and impatient with protocol. His riding crop tapped once against his boot as he adjusted his garrison cap, scanning the scene with pale, unblinking blue eyes.

Before Patton could say another word, a sharply dressed officer approached at a brisk, almost theatrical pace.

An aide entered carrying a folded signal dispatch stamped with urgent priority markings from Allied High Command.

"From Eisenhower's staff, sir."

Patton took the message without a word.

The typed transmission was brief, direct, and unmistakably operational:

German armored formations remain concentrated north and east of the Seine. Deception operations continue successful. Washington authorizes immediate expansion planning for renewed cross-Channel operations. Further directives forthcoming.

Patton stood motionless as his eyes moved across the final line.

For several seconds, the room remained silent except for the distant clatter of typewriters beyond the tent walls.

Then he folded the dispatch carefully and looked toward the wall map of France.

"Good," he said quietly. "Now we finish it properly."

The European campaign, still reeling from the failed Normandy landings and the costly evacuation that followed, now stood at a dangerous crossroads.

Patton remained motionless for a moment, staring across the wall map of France.

Beyond the Channel, the war was shifting again.

And for the first time since Normandy collapsed, George Patton could feel momentum beginning to return.

Fort Myer War Room — The Next Morning

The war room at Fort Myer sweltered under the July sun. Electric fans droned in the corners, struggling against the stagnant air. The scent of sweat, paper, and pipe smoke hung heavy. Brass buttons glinted under overhead lights. Officers had long since shed their jackets, sleeves rolled high, brows damp.

At the head of the table stood General Patton—stripped to his khaki shirt, his Colt holstered at his hip, steel helmet gleaming beside a spread of maps. Northern France sprawled before them in paper and ink. Colored pins marked the lost beaches of the June invasion. Red circles wrapped the landing zones like bruises.

He didn't waste time.

"Gentlemen," Patton began, his voice clipped, low, and firm, "we failed in June because we hesitated. We sent brave boys ashore with no armor, no reserves, and no teeth. We threw fists at a man with a machine gun."

Silence fell. No one moved.

Colonel Oscar Koch, his wiry, no-nonsense intelligence chief, leaned in over the map. "The Germans had days to fill the gaps. Once their artillery zeroed the beaches, we were boxed in."

"Exactly," Patton snapped. "Next time, we don't wait for a beachhead. We make it—with armor."

The officers exchanged glances. Brigadier General Hobart "Hap" Gay, ever the quiet backbone at Patton's side, tapped his pen slowly on a leather-bound notepad.

"How early are you thinking, George?" he asked, his voice low.

Patton picked up a red pencil and drew a quick, brutal line across the map, slicing near Quinéville.

"Higgins boats go in first. Infantry hits with airborne cover under continuous naval barrage. No pauses. No silences. Destroyers fire until our boys are halfway up the beach. I want them to feel like thunder walks beside them."

Koch looked up, brow furrowed. "And the tanks?"

"No delay," Patton said. "LSTs land within the hour. Packed—Shermans, ammo, fuel, engineers, bulldozers, half-tracks. I don't want to see a clean patch of sand when we're done. We hit them with a reverse Blitzkrieg. Speed, pressure, chaos."

Major General Leland Hobbs shifted in his seat. "The Navy's going to balk. They'll say LSTs are too slow, too exposed. We could lose half before they touch shore."

Patton didn't blink. "Better to lose steel than blood. If we wait for the perfect wave, we lose the war. We drape the landing zone with every Thunderbolt, every Mustang, every Marauder we've got. Air cover thick as smoke."

Captain Cummings, the Navy liaison, looked doubtful. "Even with good weather, that's a hell of a bet. One bad swell…"

"War is a bet, Captain," Patton cut in. "But I don't gamble blind. I've studied Jerry's tempo. They move like a metronome. Break that rhythm, and they crumble."

Koch tapped a German division marker. "If we hit fast, we might catch them mid-rotation. Their armor's still redeploying after June. Their flanks are thin."

Patton stepped toward the open window. Outside, the Potomac shimmered under the heavy morning sky. A bird wheeled overhead, silent.

"This is our second chance," he said quietly. "And I'll be damned if I let Europe rot under a boot because we're afraid of some waves."

The White House — Three Days Later

The Oval Office was dim, curtains drawn against the furnace-like summer sun. A clock ticked with slow determination on the mantle. President Franklin D. Roosevelt sat behind his desk, hands steepled, shoulders hunched beneath the weight of two oceans of war.

Patton stood before him, still dusty from field briefings. Patton stood before him, still dusty from field briefings, his peaked cap tucked beneath one arm, boots polished and posture rigid.

Beside Roosevelt stood General George C. Marshall, arms folded, his face granite still.

"I understand your urgency, George," Marshall said. "But this isn't Sicily. This is the Western Front. You're proposing to land tanks within the first hour."

Patton nodded. "Yes, sir. Because if we don't, we repeat June. And if we repeat June, we lose."

Roosevelt leaned forward slightly, the shadows hollowing his cheeks. "And what makes your plan different?"

"Speed. Timing. Force," Patton replied, voice modulated. "In June, we landed men—then waited too long for armor. That gave Jerry time to dig in. This time, we land as one. Infantry, tanks, engineers—shoulder to shoulder. The smoke won't even clear before Shermans are rolling inland."

Marshall sighed. "Churchill's already worried. The Navy too."

Patton's jaw flexed. "Let Churchill worry about speeches. Let me worry about the goddamned beach. Give me two hundred LSTs, full bombardment, air cover. I'll be in Cherbourg in seventy-two hours."

Roosevelt tapped ash from his cigarette, his eyes searching Patton's face.

"You ever hear the story of the Tokyo raid?" Patton asked suddenly. "A Navy carrier launching Army bombers in '42. Crazy. Impossible. But you said yes. And Doolittle's boys took off. They hit Tokyo. Gave us hope when we had none."

Roosevelt looked up, eyes glinting.

Patton didn't flinch. "Sir, I'm asking you to break doctrine again. Let armor lead. Let me hit Hitler the way that skipper hit Hirohito—fast, loud, and where they least expect it."

A long pause.

Roosevelt turned to Marshall. "General?"

Marshall's voice was calm, measured. "If he pulls it off, it breaks the stalemate."

Roosevelt looked back at Patton, the moment stretching between them like taut wire.

"You'll have your LSTs. Your window. Your barrage," he said.

Then, after a beat, quieter: "God help you, George. If this fails, there won't be another shot."

Patton straightened, saluted with crisp finality.

"That's all I needed, sir."

He turned.

"George," Roosevelt called softly.

Patton stopped.

"Make them bleed."

A grin crept across the general's face—feral, quiet, assured.

"I intend to."

Chapter 19

The Devil Dogs and the Lion

★★★ Before returning to England, General George S. Patton had one final meeting to attend. The sharp cadence of his boots echoed through the Pentagon's E-ring corridor like rifle fire on concrete—crisp, unwavering, and purposeful. Every step sounded like defiance wrapped in discipline. Officers stepped aside without prompting, not merely out of protocol but instinct. Patton moved like a man who didn't ask permission. He simply advanced.

Outside, Washington broiled. July pressed down with feverish weight, turning uniforms into damp second skins and tempers into lit fuses. Humidity clung to the building like a second coat of paint, seeping through the limestone walls and frosting every pane of glass with a dull haze. But inside, the Pentagon was a refrigerated bunker of war plans and whispers. Roaring ceiling vents pumped out cold, recycled air, making the place feel both sterile and intense.

Patton's khaki field uniform was immaculate, though a sweat-darkened crease marked his collar. His leather Sam Browne belt was polished to a mirror sheen, boots black and sharp enough to slice through red tape. His silver stars gleamed under fluorescent lighting—three on each shoulder strap. Even in this fortress of hierarchy and friction, presentation mattered.

A commander had to look like war—especially when war wasn't going well.

He hadn't been summoned for rebuke. The disaster at Normandy had not been his doing. That burden belonged elsewhere—on the shoulders of Eisenhower and his risk-averse coterie of consensus-makers. No, Patton had been called home because the gamble had failed. The Atlantic Wall had not crumbled beneath Allied bravado. It had held—like a rusted iron gate slammed shut in the face of liberation.

The beaches of Normandy had become slaughterhouses. Omaha and Utah—names once etched on planning maps with hopeful ink—were now blood-choked surf zones. Sword, Juno, and Gold had fared no better. British and Canadian regiments were pinned by interlocking arcs of machine gun fire. Armor foundered in the storm-swollen sea. Landing craft overturned or were gutted on steel hedgehogs. The English Channel, once envisioned as a springboard to freedom, had become a graveyard of wreckage and still-sinking dreams.

What had been promised as a thunderclap of liberation now looked like a rout.

And the world was watching.

Patton descended a narrow stairwell two levels below street level into the War Department's secure briefing room. The chill hit him immediately. The air here was still and cool, tinged with stale coffee, chalk dust, and the hum of electricity. A single overhead fan spun lazily, like it, too, had lost its enthusiasm for the war.

General George C. Marshall stood near the tall, narrow window that offered a hazy view of the Potomac. His uniform jacket was unbuttoned, and his hands were clasped behind his back. Behind him, the massive wall map of Europe glowed in muted amber and crimson hues. Tiny red lights blinked across northern France, forming a constellation of failure—each one a dead spear tip, a failed beachhead, a buried platoon.

Marshall didn't turn.

"Patton," he said, voice even, unreadable.

Patton halted just inside the doorway, snapped his heels together, and waited.

"You're going back," Marshall continued. "You'll have command of the Third Army. Possibly the Ninth as well, if we can peel it from Bradley. You've got weeks, not months, to prepare. No more. Eisenhower remains Supreme Allied Commander. But this next invasion—planning, preparation, execution—that's yours. Ike's already prioritizing the men and equipment you requested. Anything else?"

Patton's jaw twitched. "Understood. I'll need armor. Engineers. Air cover. And—"

He paused just a beat. Then said it.

"Marines."

Marshall turned at that. Slowly.

His face, carved with fatigue, bore the erosion of five years of high command. His mouth tightened to a line beneath pale, calculating eyes.

"Excuse me?" he asked. The tone was flat and dangerous.

"Marines," Patton repeated, slower this time. "A few battalions. A reinforced brigade if I can get it. Not for line assaults. For precision targets—fortified ports, airfield seizures, direct ship-to-shore strikes. Commando raids, if need be."

Marshall's jaw flexed. His fingers curled behind his back.

"There will never be a Marine in Europe as long as I'm Chief of Staff."

It was the line Patton expected. Interservice rivalry between the Army and the Marine Corps had existed since the Revolution. But the bitterness now ran deeper—fueled by Pacific headlines, media glamour, and the politics of victory.

"Sir, this isn't about protocol," Patton said. "It's about readiness. We can't afford another meat grinder. We need men trained for this. Ship-to-shore doctrine. Shock and seizure. The Marines were born in it."

Marshall walked slowly to the map, his finger tracing the jagged French coastline like a surgeon preparing to cut.

"The Army will do the job," he said. "It always has. The Marines have their war—in the Pacific. Europe is Army ground."

Patton didn't flinch.

"And yet Marines are already here. Not in divisions, no—but present. Embassy details. Naval legations. Aboard battleships. Manning flak guns. Running fire control. OSS operatives—drawn from the Corps—conducting sabotage in occupied France. They're behind enemy lines now."

Marshall said nothing. He stared at the blinking red lights on the coast—each one a scar.

"There are Marine aviators in Algiers," Patton pressed. "MAG-51. Carrier-qualified. Precision-trained. They were part of Project Danny. Corsairs armed with Tiny Tim rockets. The only serious plan we had to knock out the V-1 launch sites."

Marshall finally turned again.

"That plan was shelved," he snapped. "Too complicated. Politically untenable. The Navy wouldn't commit the carriers. The Corps stood down."

"They saluted," Patton replied. "But they didn't agree."

Silence followed—thick and brittle.

The hum of the wall map's transformer vibrated faintly under their boots. Distant footsteps above barely registered. Time was elastic in war rooms—measured not by clocks, but by consequences.

Marshall's voice, when it came again, had softened—but it carried more weight.

"We're straining, George. The alliance is threadbare. The British are exhausted. The Canadians are gutted. The Free French are split between three governments that barely recognize each other."

He stepped back from the map and leaned against the edge of the desk, eyes clouded.

"And now… Monty."

Patton's brow lifted. "What about him?"

Marshall exhaled. "Montgomery's heard about your return. He's livid. Gathering every Commando unit left in theater. He's forming a new strike force under his direct control. Wants to lead the next counter-invasion. His own plan. His own troops. He's torching Britain's last manpower reserves to do it."

Patton's expression didn't change, but a hint of amusement lit his eyes.

"Monty loves an audience," he said. "But he won't lead an armored breakout through France. Not unless he can walk every mile in advance and have tea waiting in every farmhouse."

Marshall's mouth twitched, almost a smile. "Be that as it may, if the next landing fails, there won't be a breakout. Not for you. Not for him. Not for anyone."

The sky beyond the window was turning the color of bruised slate. A summer storm was coming—dark clouds piling like artillery shells over the Virginia hills. The Potomac below looked restless, wide and gray.

"I called you back," Marshall said, his voice quiet now, "because you know how to rally men. You move fast. You build momentum. But we don't need a maverick."

He turned toward Patton fully.

"We need a hammer."

Patton's reply was steady, unwavering. "Then give me the forge."

Marshall didn't answer. But neither did he object.

The room seemed to settle into silence again.

The Marines were off the table. For now.

But Patton never fought on just one front.

Later That Afternoon – Arlington Hall Annex

The heat outside hit like a body blow. A new wave of it had rolled in off the river, thick as tar and twice as suffocating. Civilian clerks fanned themselves with folders and open briefcases. Uniformed men moved through the glare like sleepwalkers, eyes half-lidded against the punishing sun. Even the great American flags that hung above the columns of Arlington Hall drooped, too tired to flutter.

Patton entered his temporary office in the annex, stripped off his tunic, rolled his sleeves, and poured himself a glass of water that tasted faintly of brass.

Then he summoned his Chief of Staff.

There would be no memos. No paper trail. No names.

The instructions were given quietly, one sentence at a time, each more surgical than the last.

They would identify Marine security personnel posted to neutral embassies in Spain, Portugal, and Switzerland—men with combat training buried under diplomatic titles. They would reach out—discreetly—to OSS officers with Marine backgrounds embedded behind enemy lines. They would locate Marine fire control detachments aboard naval task forces in the Atlantic, men officially assigned to gunnery stations, but trained for ship-to-shore seizure.

They would build a shadow roster.

Unofficially, the next invasion would be Army-led.

But Patton had no intention of leaving the Marines behind.

Not in colors—but in blood. Not in name—but in firepower.

Because in war, permission was one thing.

Victory—that was something else entirely.

Chapter 20

Steel Before the Shore

★★★ The wind off the Channel carried the sharp tang of salt and seaweed, tugging at the edges of the canvas tent crouched low among the Cornish hedgerows. The tent, one of a dozen like it, blended into the surrounding moorland with netting and earth-toned fabric that rippled like camouflage skin. It stood just inside a double perimeter of barbed wire, guard towers, and patrolling MPs armed with tommy guns. The entire compound was an enigma, buried in the green folds of the English countryside. No signs pointed the way. No paved roads led in. To the outside world, it didn't exist.

The nearest hamlet had been emptied under the cover of a fabricated gas leak. RAF flight corridors were quietly redrawn to divert reconnaissance away from this section of Cornwall. Even friendly units with the proper clearance found themselves rerouted without explanation. What happened here was not just secret—it was sacred. A final chance wrapped in layers of silence.

The Allies had many secrets. But none as volatile, as dangerous, or as audacious as what General George S. Patton was assembling in this forgotten corner of England.

He had just returned from Washington, D.C., under an umbrella of secrecy so dense it rivaled the cloak-and-dagger work of agents operating deep in the Reich. His journey back across the Atlantic was itself a small miracle of operational deception. First, a flight aboard a military C-54 to Newfoundland. Then a blacked-out freighter under civilian guise, slipping past U-boats under radio silence, escorted not by destroyers but by fog and fortune. The general who had once mocked camouflage now lived by it.

And for good reason.

The previous operation—June 6, the great Allied invasion of Normandy—had been publicly described as a temporary strategic reversal, softened by newspapers and carefully managed statements from Allied high command. But to Patton, it had been a disaster narrowly rescued from complete annihilation.

The headlines spoke of "heroic withdrawal" and "preserved combat strength," while the reality had been slower, bloodier, and far more dangerous. Entire units had vanished in the hedgerows and surf. Timetables shattered. Objectives collapsed. The Atlantic Wall had not been broken.

It had held.

The cost in lives had been enormous, and in momentum: incalculable.

Patton had torn through Washington like a battering ram in olive drab. He argued, demanded, condemned. He flayed assumptions with a general's precision and a butcher's clarity. In meetings with Roosevelt and Marshall, he laid out his vision—steel before strategy, tempo before caution. Give him the reins. Give him the firepower. Give him one last chance to make the enemy retreat all the way to Berlin.

Fast. Furious. Final.

Now, back on British soil, Patton carried more than just command orders. He carried the weight of that promise. And the war's unspoken ultimatum.

There would not be another chance.

Inside the command tent, the air was taut—not hot, but pressurized, like a boiler ticking toward detonation. Oil lamps flickered behind sandbag-lined flaps, casting long, twitching shadows across a field table covered in a sprawl of dispatches, updated battle maps, and grease-pencil diagrams redrawn until the paper frayed. The scent was familiar: damp wool, stale coffee, and the faint metallic tinge of gun oil. Everything about the space declared readiness—not for planning, but for execution.

Patton stood hunched over a map of northern France, his gloved hands braced against the folding table. His uniform bore the creases and salt marks of hard travel. Dust from the Cornish cliffs clung to his boots. His jaw was clenched, his skin pale beneath the brim of his helmet liner. Only his eyes betrayed no fatigue—two flint-colored torches, locked on the jagged coastline of Normandy.

"We're not repeating June," he growled without looking up. "No more half-measures. No more drift. We hit, and we break them. For good."

Across from him stood Major General Otto P. "Opie" Weyland, commander of tactical air support. One of the few men Patton trusted to speak directly, Weyland had earned his stripes in North Africa and Sicily. His flight jacket hung unzipped, his sleeves rolled. His face was sun-weathered and alert, jaw stubbled, boots muddy from recon visits to forward airfields.

"You'll have it, George," Weyland said. "Squadrons are locked in from Wiltshire to Essex. Thunderbolts are staged for low-level strafing. Lightnings are loaded for bridge strikes and munitions depots. Pilots have rehearsed every flight path—twice. Your armor won't hit a hedgerow without my boys clearing it first."

Patton looked up. His eyes were bloodshot, but sharp as razors.

"I don't want a clear path," he snapped. "I want a scorched one. I want German reserves in flames before my tanks cross the tree line. I want panzers burning in their staging grounds. If I see smoke, it better be from their fuel trucks—not from one of my stalled Shermans."

Weyland didn't blink. "Understood. But I'll need precision updates. If your lead elements get ahead and don't report in, we're either dropping on empty fields—or on your own damn tanks."

Patton gave a thin, feral smile. "You'll get precision. I'll lash a damn radio to my aide's helmet if I have to. You cover my flanks, I'll crack their spine."

Weyland folded his arms, not in defiance but solidarity. "Luftwaffe's weak but not dead. If they catch wind of your push, they'll toss their last squadrons at your spearpoints. Especially once you cross the second ridge."

"Good," Patton said flatly. "You make them duck. I'll make them bleed. But I won't halt this army for air clearance. We slow down, we lose the bite."

"I'll embed forward air controllers with your vanguards. Jeep-mounted if necessary. They'll call in targets from the lead elements. No waiting."

Patton nodded once. "That's how we win. Tell your boys to stay with us—or get out of our way. If they fall behind, they better hope Jerry finds them before I do."

Weyland's voice dropped a half pitch. "Air power can't plant flags, George. That's your job."

Patton straightened. His whole frame seemed to stiffen.

"Damn right it is. But you light the way, and I'll drive that flag straight to the Rhine."

At that moment, the canvas flap lifted. A gust of salt wind entered, along with the sharp scent of peat and sea. A tall figure stepped inside—a silhouette of precision. Navy blue coat, gold trim, cap in hand. Vice Admiral Harold Burrough Ramsay.

Royal Navy. Iron-willed. A strategist as precise as a naval chronometer.

"Apologies for the delay," Ramsay said, voice clipped, vowels tight. "Intercepted E-boat chatter late last night. Repositioning toward Boulogne. They're shifting. That means they're listening."

"Good," Patton said, still leaning over the map. "Let them listen. When the guns start, they'll realize they weren't nervous enough."

He gestured at the Normandy coastlines drawn in meticulous detail.

"This time, we hit hard. You start shelling before first light. I want those coastal batteries dead before my boys leave the sand. Then bring in your destroyers. Close. Real close. If Jerry shoves us back, I want him torched where he stands."

Ramsay's brow lifted at the audacity. But he nodded.

"Six thousand yards. Any closer and we risk taking shells ourselves. But within that perimeter, if they rise to resist, we'll flatten them with naval artillery. My cruisers begin bombardment three hours prior to H-Hour.

In conjunction with His Majesty's carrier aircraft, our land-based British and Canadian fighters, fighter-bombers, and heavy bombers will unleash hell on the German coastal defenses.

Aircraft and naval assets are already being diverted from the Mediterranean. Their squadrons will launch as your forces press inland.

London's taken a considerable risk on this, General.

Let's make it count."

Patton locked eyes with him.

"I want naval liaisons in the first wave. Direct comms. No delays. If my officers call for naval fire, I want shells in the air, not paperwork on the way."

Ramsay unfolded his own chart, nodding. "Fire control teams will be embedded with your lead regiments. Radios tuned. Strike flexibility authorized through the second terrain ridge. But beyond that, the tempo becomes yours. We'll hold the sea behind you. The ground… that's your war."

Patton tapped a red X near Caen.

"I'm not interested in holding. I'm interested in rupturing. I'll drive through the Atlantic Wall and keep going until fuel or ammo runs out. And then I'll take theirs."

Ramsay studied him for a moment—calculating, appraising. Then a faint smile touched the corners of his mouth.

"Very well. Just don't count on the Channel staying quiet. The Kriegsmarine still has teeth. If they get brave, we counter without hesitation."

"That's all I needed to hear."

Patton straightened. His presence, even rumpled, seemed to expand. He looked between the two men—air and sea commanders—then toward the canvas wall where the wind flickered shadows like flames.

"Weyland gives me the sky. Ramsay gives me the sea. I'll take the rest."

And with that, he stepped outside.

The sky above the moor was the color of hammered steel, thick clouds rolling inland from the sea. Somewhere offshore, the growl of destroyer engines echoed against the cliffs. A gull wheeled overhead, its cry swallowed by the breeze.

Behind him, the war was still being drafted in ink.

Ahead of him, it would be written in steel, fire—and blood.

Chapter 21

Invasion Planning Brief

★★★ The wind outside had stiffened, tugging at guy lines and snapping canvas flaps with impatient cracks. A sergeant ducked into the tent, saluted sharply. "Briefing group is assembled, sir."

Patton didn't respond immediately. He stood in the doorway, eyes sweeping the moor—as if searching the horizon for ghosts. Then, without a word, he turned on his heel and strode down the gravel path toward a stone barn that had been converted into a secure war room. The MPs at the door stepped aside without a glance, pulling it open to reveal a low-ceilinged chamber lit by flickering overhead lamps and the bluish glow of a massive wall map plastered with color-coded pins, movement arrows, and German unit markers.

Inside, a dozen senior officers waited—American, British, Canadian. A fusion of uniforms, accents, and egos. Behind them stood aides and liaison officers, notebooks in hand, eyes sharp. The room fell silent the instant Patton entered.

He said nothing at first. He moved to the front of the room, peeling off his gloves as he studied the map. Then he turned to face the room, letting the silence stretch just a moment longer than comfort allowed.

"When this is over," he said at last, voice low and deliberate, "I want the world to forget Normandy. I want them to remember this."

He let the sentence settle, then jabbed a finger toward the chalkboard beside the map. On it, the operation's codename was scrawled in block letters:

OPERATION VALIANT SWORD

"We didn't come to nibble at Europe's edges. We came to crush the beast's throat. June sixth was a costly lesson. This—this is the correction. And we will not fail twice."

He turned toward the map and pointed to a coastal sector south of Le Havre.

"We land here. Pre-dawn. Under cover of rolling bombardment. Weyland's bombers will tear the arteries. Ramsay's cruisers will gut the defenses. And then we hit the sand—fast, hard, and everywhere. No staggered waves. No bottlenecks. Armor follows infantry in the first hour. No more sitting in the surf."

A hand rose. Brigadier General Carlton Ames—logistics lead.

"General Patton, our supply estimates suggest—"

"I'm not interested in what they suggest, General," Patton snapped. "We take the beach, we secure the causeways, and we move. If we can't keep up with our own armor, we'll be driving captured German trucks by noon."

Ames lowered his eyes. Nothing more needed saying.

Patton turned back to the map, eyes narrowing.

"Inland terrain is hedgerow country—tight, choking, perfect for ambush. We don't dig in. We plow through. Each corps is assigned a corridor. You are not to deviate unless your entire division is wiped out—and if that happens, you'll still find a way forward."

He motioned to two aides, who stepped forward and unrolled transparent overlays. Aerial recon photos followed—rail lines, artillery nests, suspected Panzer staging zones.

"Rommel pulled his reserves toward Calais last month. Let him. The Krauts don't believe lightning can strike twice. We'll prove them wrong."

From the far side of the room came a calm, clipped voice—Major Thomas Levin, intelligence liaison.

"Ultra decrypts indicate increased movement of the 116th Panzer Division south of Rouen. They may not be fully in the dark."

"Let them wonder," Patton said. "They won't know where—or when. By the time they react, we'll already be cutting through their arteries."

He paused. Then his voice dropped, quiet but burning.

"You all know what's at stake. If we lose this—this one shot—we give Hitler another year. Another winter. Maybe worse. If we win, we break his hold on the West. We open the road to Paris. To Berlin. To victory."

Patton moved around the table, eyes locking with each commander.

"Gentlemen, I don't believe in fighting for inches. I believe in destroying the enemy's capacity to fight—utterly. That's what this is. We don't land to hold ground. We land to kill the enemy. And we keep moving until nothing stands in our way."

The air in the room had changed. Even the British officers—stoic and reserved—now leaned in. Behind them, aides scribbled furiously, transcribing words they knew might one day be carved into stone.

Patton looked left.

"General Moore. You lead the central beach assault. You'll have armor in the first thirty minutes. Your infantry must punch deep enough for tanks to break through. If you falter, the whole front collapses."

Moore, a scarred Texan from the Africa campaign, nodded once. "We won't falter, sir."

"To your right, General Hargrove's engineers will clear and hold the causeways. I want armor routes cleared by H plus ninety. Every minute beyond that, we lose momentum."

Patton shifted to Brigadier Simmons, the Canadian commander.

"Your units take the eastern flank. That's our hinge. If the Germans counterattack, it'll come from your sector. I want your artillery dug in and already calling targets before boots even hit the sand."

Simmons nodded. "We'll be ready."

A tall figure stepped forward from the back—a lean, hawk-eyed British officer in Commando green, insignia subdued. Major Arthur Calloway, attached as special liaison for Allied raiding operations. Patton gestured toward him.

"Major Calloway's men will insert ahead of the landing. They'll knock out shore batteries and radar sites before the first wave makes contact. We hit with surprise, and they hit in the dark."

Calloway's voice was crisp. "Target packages are finalized. We deploy four hours prior to H-Hour. Close coordination with your naval fire teams. We'll keep the seafront blind and bleeding."

Near the side wall, a square-jawed Marine officer stood silently beside a communications aide. His uniform bore no insignia other than rank—Captain—and a nameplate: Colter. He caught Patton's eye. No words were exchanged. None were needed.

Captain Colter's detachment—drawn discreetly from embassy guards, shipboard complements, and Marine Raiders now folded into the OSS—would not be listed in official orders. But they would be there. Quietly clearing bunkers. Sabotaging fuel dumps. Marking targets for airstrikes. The kind of work no army owned, but Patton had made part of his plan.

Patton stepped back. "I'll be with the lead armor. Not in the rear. Not in an ops shack five miles back. There. On the front. This war ends with boots—not memos."

A murmur passed through the room. At the back, Ramsay and Weyland had entered quietly, arms crossed, listening.

Patton turned to them now, voice rising.

"We've got the sky. We've got the sea. Now we take the land. Operation Valiant Sword isn't a maneuver. It's the blade that'll cut Europe loose. And if any of you think you'll hide behind procedure when the bullets start flying, I'll personally send you back to Washington, London, and Ottawa wrapped in your own red tape."

He stopped, exhaled.

"Dismissed. Make your preparations."

The room broke—some officers murmuring quietly, others filing out in silence, expressions tight with purpose. Aides followed, pages in hand, radios already sparking to life. Outside, clouds had gathered low on the horizon. The wind had shifted—from sea to land.

Patton remained alone at the map. His hand rested on a marked beachhead—soon to be bloodied, but soon, if they moved fast enough, brutal enough, bold enough, to be Allied ground.

Behind him, Ramsay spoke.

"You made them believe."

Patton didn't turn. "Good. Now let's make the enemy believe it too."

Chapter 22

The Measure of Men

★★★ Rain tapped insistently against the leaded windows of the stone farmhouse Montgomery had requisitioned as his temporary headquarters. Outside, the sky was the color of iron filings, and the fields of Hampshire lay sodden beneath a slow-moving fog. Inside, only the rhythmic ticking of a wall clock and the soft rustling of maps disturbed the silence.

Field Marshal Bernard Law Montgomery stood at the window, hands clasped behind his back, posture ramrod straight even in stillness. A cup of tea—untouched—cooled on the map table behind him. His cap lay beside it, perfectly aligned. Order was Montgomery's religion, and in his world, every object—and every man—had a place.

He didn't turn when his chief of staff, Major General Freddie de Guingand, entered the room with a dispatch folder in hand.

"It's official, sir," de Guingand said quietly. "SHAEF has approved Patton's operation. Valiant Sword is greenlit. Launch date to be announced, but likely within ten days."

Montgomery exhaled through his nose, sharp and slow.

"Of course they have."

He turned at last, taking the folder from de Guingand with gloved fingers. Inside were the details—Patton's revised beach sectors, Weyland's strike coordination, Ramsay's naval support timeline. He flipped through the pages, jaw tightening.

"Valiant Sword," he said aloud, dryly. "Sounds like something from a cowboy serial."

De Guingand didn't reply.

Montgomery set the folder down and crossed to the hearth. He didn't need to read the plan. He could feel its shape from a distance—fast, direct, improvised. Maneuver warfare by impulse. His lips pressed into a line.

"Does Roosevelt even understand what he's signed off on? Does Eisenhower?"

De Guingand hesitated. "The Prime Minister is aware, sir. He's been briefed. He... supports it. Though privately, he's expressed some concern."

Montgomery turned sharply.

"Concern won't hold a line, Freddie. What Churchill's endorsed is a gamble. One so reckless it borders on criminal."

De Guingand cleared his throat. "With respect, sir... Patton sees this as redemption for June 6."

Montgomery's eyes flared.

"Redemption? Is that what they're calling it now?"

He moved back toward the table and opened the folder again, flipping pages with sudden intensity.

"He's even requested British Commandos for his forward assault groups," de Guingand added, almost ruefully. "Wants them embedded with American Rangers. Apparently, the Canadians signed off as well."

Montgomery's hand paused over a page. His voice dropped.

"And no one thought to consult British high command," he said coldly. "That's the measure of it now. Borrowing our crown jewels to sharpen an American bayonet."

Another silence.

"I commanded that invasion, Freddie. Not Ike. Not Patton. Me. And I know how thin our gains were. Those beaches were barely held. Now Patton wants to throw another army at them like a battering ram, with no reserve, no depth, no patience. And they'll call it victory because it looks good on paper."

A soft knock interrupted them. An aide entered—a young captain holding a communiqué.

"Sir. General Eisenhower requests a coordination meeting. 1900 hours. Location: Southwick House."

Montgomery waved him out. "Very well."

When the door closed, he looked again at de Guingand.

"This is being taken from me, Freddie. Bit by bit. The Americans are no longer junior partners—they've taken the wheel. First the air war. Then logistics. Now the ground offensive."

De Guingand spoke carefully. "If it succeeds—"

Montgomery cut him off.

"If it succeeds, Patton becomes a hero. I become a footnote."

He let that hang—not bitterly, just as fact.

But then, unexpectedly, his voice softened—threaded with something older, deeper.

"Do you remember what I said in North Africa? That this wasn't just about winning battles. It was about imposing will. On the enemy. On the men. On the war itself."

"Yes, sir," de Guingand said.

Montgomery turned back to the rain-blurred window. Somewhere out in that gray murk, Patton's armor was assembling. Eisenhower was nodding. Churchill was smiling through clenched teeth.

"And now," he murmured, "I must impose my will on chaos."

Later That Evening — Southwick House

The long oak table in the briefing hall gleamed under warm lamps, surrounded by the commanders of two empires. Montgomery entered last—not from discourtesy, but from design. Patton was already seated, legs crossed, gloves resting on the table like trophies.

Montgomery did not sit. He studied the central map.

"Your corridors are exposed," he said without greeting.

Patton didn't look up. "So were the ones on June 6."

Montgomery's brow twitched. "I favored breadth, not bluster."

Patton raised his eyes. "And the Germans favored slaughter. I'm not here to bleed slowly, Monty. I'm here to win."

Eisenhower stepped in quickly. "Gentlemen, there's no time for another war inside this one. This operation goes forward. You will coordinate."

Montgomery gave a stiff nod. "Of course, Supreme Commander. But coordination doesn't mean surrendering judgment."

Patton stood, gathering his gloves with a calm finality.

"No. It means acting. See you on the beach, Monty. I'll be the one moving forward."

He walked out, each bootstep echoing like distant gunfire.

Montgomery didn't move.

"The man will break something," he said quietly. "I only pray it's not Europe."

Chapter 23

Old Soldiers and Quiet Truths

★★★ Normandy, France – July 12, 1944. The sea was just a faint whisper now, a hush beyond the low dunes and gun emplacements. In the dying light of the July evening, the Normandy coastline appeared almost peaceful—its treachery tucked beneath a veil of mist rolling in with the tide. Field Marshal Erwin Rommel stood near the open window of his commandeered villa outside Vimont, Normandy, listening to the muffled rustle of sea grass and the muted clatter of distant artillery crews rechecking their positions. He had recently returned from a celebratory event in Berlin, commemorating Germany's victory in repelling the Allied invasion on June 6th.

Inside, Lieutenant Colonel Ernst Warnecke lit a cigarette, the tip flaring in the gloom before the smoke curled upward and joined the draft along the timbered ceiling. The room was austere: two iron cots along one wall, a desk buried in maps and communiqués, and a pair of creaking wooden chairs facing a small hearth where a low fire cracked. On the far wall hung a crooked oil painting of a spring orchard, left behind by the villa's previous owners. Neither man paid it any attention.

Rommel's hands were clasped behind his back, his tunic collar undone, shoulders drawn tight with fatigue. His face—once bronze from North African winds—was now pale, drawn by strain, sharpened by weeks of uncertainty. The weight of failure lay heavy in the Normandy air, but it was not German failure. Not yet.

"They'll come again," Rommel said quietly. "Not today. Not tomorrow. But soon."

Warnecke exhaled slowly. "No question about it. They didn't bleed out at Caen just to turn back for good."

Rommel nodded without turning. "June 6 gave us a temporary reprieve. But it also gave them a lesson. The next attack will be different. Better planned. More aggressive. If I were them, I'd send Patton."

Warnecke grunted in agreement. "Patton's name keeps surfacing in intercepted traffic. And Allied supply traffic across southern England has increased sharply. They're not retreating—they're preparing for another blow."

Rommel finally turned from the window, reaching for the battered tin coffee pot on the stove. He poured two cups, black and thick, and handed one to Warnecke.

They sat without ceremony, settling into the chairs with the slow gravity of men used to colder benches and harder fields. The ticking of the mantle clock filled the silence for a moment.

"You've seen the latest reports from Berlin?" Rommel asked.

Warnecke nodded. "Garbled. Rushed. More pronouncements than plans. Some still believe the June failure means the Allies have given up."

Rommel shook his head. "Idiots. We didn't defeat them. We disoriented them. And they're already adapting."

"I've reviewed the dispositions of Fifteenth Army in the Pas de Calais," Warnecke said, tapping ash into a tin tray. "They're still holding them in reserve—waiting for a phantom second landing that's never coming."

Rommel's voice darkened. "Hitler's obsession with Calais will destroy us. I've begged to reposition the panzer reserves closer to the Cotentin Peninsula. Berlin refuses. Rundstedt won't press it. They want miracles, not strategy."

"You've built what you could here," Warnecke said. "But concrete and steel only buy time."

Rommel gave a short nod. "Time is all we have."

He leaned forward, warming his hands on the ceramic mug. "I asked you here, Ernst, not just because you understand defenses. I need a man who sees what's coming—and doesn't lie to himself about it."

Warnecke's expression didn't change, but his voice softened. "You already know, Erwin. The Reich is crumbling under its own weight. We both see it. But the uniforms won't allow us to say it out loud."

Rommel tilted his head. "Say it anyway."

Warnecke took a breath. "We've delayed them. Not defeated them. The next attack will break through—if not here, then to the west, near Saint-Lô. And when they come, it won't be tentative. They'll throw everything behind it. Armor. Airpower. Logistics. A second failure is not an option for them."

Rommel looked down at the steam rising from his cup. "And we are not ready."

"No," Warnecke said flatly. "We're not."

For a while, the fire spoke more than either of them. Wood popped, sparks rose, and the smell of old smoke hung in the corners of the room.

Rommel stood again and walked to a small field chest beneath the window. He opened it and drew out a worn leather folder. From inside it, he retrieved a photograph and held it out to Warnecke.

Three men stood smiling in a sun-blasted airfield: Rommel, Warnecke, and Oberst Eduard Möller—long dead now. All younger, all hardened by the desert sun, all buoyed by the illusion of control.

"El Agheila," Rommel said quietly. "After we turned them back. We thought we were invincible."

Warnecke studied the photo, his thumb tracing the corner. "We were lucky. We mistook that for destiny."

Rommel took the photo back and placed it on the mantle beside the lopsided painting. "They still call me the Desert Fox. As if that means something anymore."

Warnecke gave a faint smile. "It means they fear your name more than your orders. That still counts for something."

Rommel turned to face him fully. "What about you, Ernst? You've had chances to step away. Safer assignments. Hamburg. Berlin. Yet here you are."

Warnecke stared into the fire. "Because you're still fighting the war as a soldier, not as a fanatic. And because there's no safety anymore—not really. I'd rather face the end here than watch it from behind a mahogany desk."

There was a knock at the door. A young adjutant entered, his helmet tucked under his arm.

"Herr Feldmarschall, the staff car is ready. Route has been cleared to Caen. Air cover not confirmed."

Rommel waved him off. The adjutant saluted and withdrew.

Rommel looked at Warnecke. "We leave at first light. Rundstedt wants a fresh assessment of the 21st Panzer positions. I'd value your eyes on the ground."

Warnecke stood and adjusted his tunic. "Then you shall have them."

Rommel smiled faintly. "Bring your notes on the Cotentin sector. If I'm right about Patton, he'll come straight through that valley west of Saint-Lô. We'll need every kilometer accounted for."

They gathered their things slowly, with the quiet rhythm of men preparing for something inevitable. Rommel paused at the door.

"One last thing."

Warnecke turned.

"If we survive this madness, I want a quiet farm. Something inland. Apples. Horses. No radios."

Warnecke nodded. "I know a place outside Kiel. Fertile ground. No politics."

Rommel gave a rare smile and opened the door.

"Then let's live long enough to get there."

They stepped into the fading night, two old soldiers beneath a silent sky, unaware that dawn would bring the scream of Spitfires and the shattering of their final conversation.

Plans fail.
Momentum decides.

Chapter 24

The Fall of the Desert Fox

★★★ Normandy, France – July 17, 1944. Normandy, France. Before dawn, a chill mist clung to the hedgerows like a shroud as Field Marshal Erwin Rommel stepped from the villa near Vimont. The Norman countryside lay hushed, fragile and still, unaware that this journey would be his last.

Rommel hadn't truly slept. The deceptive silence weighed heavy, a quiet before a storm he felt deep in his bones. The Allies had bled on the beaches months before, then vanished—warships retreating like ghosts beneath the Channel's gray cloak. In Berlin, triumphal parades and speeches celebrated a hollow victory. But Rommel's mind remained unsettled.

They had not been defeated. Only repelled. And such wounds rarely went unanswered.

The black Horch glided over narrow country lanes scarred by war—scorched fields, shattered barns—dust trailing behind like smoke from a distant blaze. Beside Rommel sat Lieutenant Colonel Ernst Warnecke, his closest confidant. Neither spoke; the weight of their recent conversation hung between them like fog.

Finally, Rommel broke the silence. "If I were them, I wouldn't strike the same beach twice."

Warnecke's eyes flicked toward him. "You think they'll come again?"

Rommel's gaze was steady. "Without question. They've regrouped, reconsidered everything. And if Patton's involved, it'll be a strike designed to finish this."

Warnecke unfolded a worn intelligence map across his lap. "Radio chatter's spiked near Portsmouth. Recon flights target the western sector—from Cherbourg to Granville. Heavy interest in Cotentin and Brittany."

Rommel leaned in, fingers tightening on the seat cushion. "That's the place to hit. Land west of Avranches, then push east through the Falaise basin. Trap the divisions between Caen and Le Mans."

Warnecke frowned. "Risk a second full invasion so soon? After June?"

Rommel exhaled, breath misting in the cold air. "They must. Hitler will believe the beaches broke them. But Ike and Patton—they see a different fight. Something bold. Unexpected. A strike to end it."

Outside, the trees bore scars of strafing runs. Overhead, the sky buzzed with an unnatural stillness.

Rommel's eyes darted upward. "Aircraft?"

Warnecke's head snapped toward the sound.

A sudden roar shattered the calm. RAF Spitfires dived low—fast and precise.

The black Horch surged, tires tearing against gravel, but escape was impossible.

Canadian Flight Lieutenant Charley Fox, spotting the dark, unmarked car, opened fire.

Rounds ripped through the treetops, tearing into hood and windshield. The driver swerved violently; the car spun out, crashing into a ditch beside a broken stone barn.

Smoke and silence swallowed the wreck.

Warnecke, blood blurring his vision, scrambled through grass to Rommel. The Field Marshal lay face down, a deep gash bleeding through his temple, his chest rising shallowly.

Minutes later, a passing patrol found them. Rommel was loaded into an ambulance, limp and pale, bound for a field hospital and then Stuttgart.

The attack was hushed, news carefully contained.

Three days passed before another explosion shattered the Reich—not from bombs but from betrayal.

July 20, 1944 – Wolfsschanze, East Prussia

A bomb beneath Hitler's conference table detonated during a routine briefing. Death followed swift and brutal. The Führer survived, shaken but alive.

What should have ended the war ignited a spiral of suspicion and reprisal. Conspirators fell, and thousands were swept into the Gestapo's net.

Rommel's name surfaced—not as a traitor, but as a critic. His whispered calls for surrender, for sanity, for mercy made him suspect.

Berlin's official line remained calm: "Field Marshal Rommel wounded in an air attack, convalescing."

But across Europe, murmurs spread: Rommel had been targeted—by fate or design.

In Stuttgart, Rommel drifted in a haze of pain and morphine. His skull fractured, spine damaged. Some moments brought lucid commands from distant deserts; others, empty silence.

Warnecke stayed by his side, shaken before returning to the front.

Without Rommel, command reverted to Rundstedt—an old soldier clinging to orders and miracles, blind to the crumbling defenses as Hitler clung to fantasies of Calais.

But the Channel was far from quiet.

Across the water, Patton and Montgomery gathered their forces for a second wave.

Operation Valiant Sword, forged in secrecy under Eisenhower's watchful eye, would strike hard, wide, and unrelenting.

Rommel, confined and guarded, would not be there to meet it.

On August 25, the steel-gray Channel thrummed with movement.

Thousands of ships churned forward beneath skies thick with Allied aircraft.

Battleships thundered their salvoes before dawn.

At a forward Allied command post near Portsmouth, General George S. Patton studied the latest report, ash flicking from his cigar.

"Rommel remains hospitalized. Condition unchanged."

Patton folded the paper, voice low and bitter.

"A hell of a way to lose a damn good enemy."

Chapter 25

When Fire Walks Ashore

★★★ August 25, 1944. In Stuttgart, Rommel lay silent beneath white sheets as the second invasion began without him—his voice stilled, just as Germany's high command fell into paralysis. Hitler's delusions blinded Berlin, and distrust fragmented what remained of strategic coherence. The generals, still basking in what they called a Normandy victory just weeks earlier, dismissed the growing Allied buildup as mere diversionary noise. What threat could possibly rise again from a French beach hundreds of miles away?

The Channel stretched flat and metallic beneath the rising sun, a silent sea of steel rippling with motion. Thousands of vessels surged eastward toward France. Mist hugged the waterline, cloaking hulls and decks in ghostly silhouette. The horizon trembled—not with thunder, but with engines of war: LSTs coughed smoke, destroyers growled into formation, landing craft sliced the chop with methodical precision.

Aboard the command ship USS Ancon, General George S. Patton stood alone at the bow rail, one gloved hand gripping the cold metal. Before him unfurled a vision once dismissed as impossible—a second invasion force, not larger in numbers, but sharper in speed and firepower. A thrust no German commander had dared to predict, much less prepare for.

This time, it would not be Normandy.

Patton's gaze swept eastward. Beyond the curtain of fog and sea lay the French coast again—this time near Montfarville, south of Le Havre, where the German Atlantic Wall had been thickened after June but not, he believed, hardened with new resolve. The Wehrmacht was weary. Its armor had been drawn elsewhere. This was the opening.

This was vengeance.

At precisely 0455 hours, the sea began to burn.

Vice Admiral Harold Burrough Ramsay's cruisers let loose a coordinated salvo, their 8-inch and 6-inch guns shaking the decks. Sheets of flame rolled down the bombardment line, joined by destroyers closing to within 6,000 yards. Their shells raked the coastline—pillboxes, gun emplacements, bunkers, radar towers—everything German and visible was drowned under thunder. Observation decks tracked the shoreline with binoculars, watching concrete erupt and trenches vanish in shockwaves of steel.

Patton's jaw tightened. "That's more like it."

Fifteen minutes later, the sky over the Channel went dark with wings.

From the west came the drone of hundreds of B-17 Flying Fortresses in staggered formation, trailing contrails in the gray morning. They roared overhead at 12,000 feet, escorted by P-51 Mustangs, and unleashed their ordnance with clinical brutality. Carpet bombing swept across a three-mile coastal band—trenches collapsed, ammunition depots vanished in flame, and road junctions turned to broken stone.

No missed targets. No guesswork. This was industrial war, delivered with surgical precision.

A pilot's voice crackled over the radio: "Target corridor obliterated. Repeat, corridor is open."

By 0520 hours, the first waves of Higgins boats surged toward the beach.

Roaring into the surf, each landing craft carried a platoon crouched in silence—faces smeared with charcoal, grips tight on rifles and grenades. Behind them, tank-carrying LCTs plowed forward, covered by barrage balloons and supported by rocket-firing destroyers. The ocean churned with smoke and machine-gun spray, but from the gunner decks of LSTs and fast attack transports, no one looked away.

These were men who remembered June.

LST-244 took a direct hit and split in two. A geyser of smoke and fire rose, but the rest did not pause.

By 0545, Allied troops hit the sand.

Elements of the 1st and 9th U.S. Infantry Divisions led the charge, supported closely by British Royal Marine Commandos and Canadian rifle teams landing in coordinated flanking sectors. The commando units had come ashore further south, targeting radar nests and forward observers. Within minutes, they had seized a ridgeline bunker and relayed coordinates back to shipboard gunners—clearing a path for Patton's main assault.

The return fire from the Germans was scattered. Blinded. Disoriented.

The German response—what there was of it—lacked coordination. Field Marshal von Kluge, who had assumed Rommel's command weeks earlier, was already gone—dead by his own hand just days ago under Hitler's suspicion of treason. His replacement, Field Marshal Walter Model, had barely arrived and was still untangling a crumbling command chain. The Western Front, for the first time in five years, had no true leader.

Patton turned to his chief of operations. "Get the Shermans moving. I want armor on that beach in fifteen minutes."

And so it came.

M4 Sherman tanks, green-gray and steaming with salt, rumbled onto blackened sand behind armored bulldozers. They fired high-explosive rounds into what few German strongpoints remained.

Along the adjoining sector, British Churchill tanks and Cromwell support vehicles thundered ashore—plowing through dragon's teeth while commandos marked paths with red smoke and phosphor flares.

Then the real fire came.

P-47 Thunderbolts streaked low from the west, screaming over the surf like mechanical hawks. Beneath their bellies hung canisters—unfamiliar to most of the troops watching below.

Napalm.

The canisters ignited on impact, exploding in sheets of liquid fire that clung to trenches and pillboxes behind the main wall. The effect was hellish—concrete bunkers boiled with flame, and enemy positions disintegrated under waves of burning gel. The smell was unique: a sick mix of rubber, fuel, and scorched flesh.

Patton had been briefed on its chemistry—naphthenic and palmitic acids blended into a sticky, incendiary gel. The Pacific had proven its worth. Now Europe would feel its wrath.

He watched as a gun nest vanished in fire and screams.

An aide beside him turned pale. "My God…"

Patton didn't flinch. "No. God sent."

By 0640 hours, two sectors of the primary seawall were breached. Engineers, hunched behind mine-clearing tanks and half-tracks, punched through barbed wire and anti-tank ditches. Smoke pots covered their movement while field radios crackled with position updates.

The invasion had become a surge.

The Germans had made two grave errors.

First: the assumption that no second assault of this scale could be attempted so soon. Their reserves had shifted north and east—toward Calais, toward Antwerp. Second: they had not imagined that the Americans would return with such coordination and cruelty. By the time the first German battalion regrouped, the beachhead was ashore—and advancing.

CIC chatter came fast now.

"Red sector secure. Push to green." "Armor crossing Point Echo. Minimal resistance." "Commandos requesting naval fire on grid 227—new target identified."

By 0810 hours, Patton himself came ashore.

His boots struck sand with deliberate force, planting him in France at last.

The wind off the water carried smoke and salt. Already, bulldozers were pushing enemy wreckage aside to clear roads inland.

A German prisoner sat nearby, bound and stunned, staring up from a shell crater. Patton looked down at him for only a moment.

"You picked the wrong war to believe in, son."

He stepped past, climbed into a waiting jeep, and ordered his driver inland. The advance command post was already three miles forward—his lead columns were on the move. Shermans. Half-tracks. Engineers. Infantry. The war machine rolled, no longer theoretical.

This time, there would be no pause. No politics. No hedgerow hesitations.

Valiant Sword had landed. And fire was walking ashore.

Chapter 26

The Fracture Beneath the Eagle

★★★ August 25, 1944 — 0930 hours. La Roche-Guyon, France. The air inside the château-turned-headquarters was brittle with silence. Field Marshal Günther von Kluge stood at the center of the operations room, shoulders slightly hunched beneath the weight of both his field coat and his responsibility. His face was pale and drawn—deep lines around the mouth betrayed a man who hadn't truly slept since the eastern rail transfers began. His eyes, fixed on a situation map already rendered obsolete, blinked only when the smoke from his cigarette curled directly into them.

Around him, aides hovered like ghosts. Radios hissed. The scratch of a pencil on a clipboard seemed unnaturally loud. But no one spoke.

Two hours earlier, the first garbled reports had cracked across the encrypted field sets—American voices on French soil. Explosions along what had been a quiet stretch of the Norman coastline. Then radio silence from multiple coastal batteries. A rising series of corroborated claims. And finally, the word no one wanted to repeat:

Invasion.

Not feints. Not raids. This was a full-scale assault.

Major Hellmuth Lang, Kluge's aide-de-camp, stepped forward, message slip in hand. His face was expressionless, but the paper trembled between his fingers.

"Field Marshal, Luftflotte 3 confirms they've lost contact with three coastal radar installations. Allied bombers struck a fifteen-kilometer stretch near Montfarville. Heavy naval shelling. P-47 Thunderbolts reported overhead. High casualties among flak and infantry units. Sir… they're saying napalm was used."

Kluge took the slip in silence. He scanned it quickly, then dropped it to the table and pressed his fingertips against his temples. The parchment map beneath his hands showed defensive positions—trenches, emplacements, fallback lines—meticulously drawn in ink now bleeding under sweat and pressure.

A wall clock ticked faintly in the corner. It seemed louder now, each second punctuating the unraveling of a front.

"How many divisions do we still have in reserve?"

Lang hesitated. "Three—perhaps four—within a hundred kilometers. Two are understrength. Most of the armor was shifted east after Antwerp, per OKW's last directive. They feared a crossing at the Scheldt."

"Of course they did," Kluge murmured. "The war has turned into a whisper game. We react to ghosts while Patton brings the thunder."

He stepped back from the table and straightened slowly, his bones audibly popping as he moved. Every instinct in him—every hard-earned lesson from the Eastern Front—told him this was the moment. Not one to delay. Not one to gamble on orders.

He looked directly at Lang.

"Call Rundstedt. Tell him I want the 21st Panzer Division moving immediately—with or without OKW's blessing. Requisition fuel from regional depots if necessary. Redirect the 352nd Infantry toward the southern corridor and seal off the interior approach routes to Caen. And Lang—mobilize every flak unit that hasn't already been vaporized and redeploy them around our command zones. If we lose command and control, this front will disintegrate in hours."

Lang nodded sharply, but his expression tightened. "Berlin will object, sir."

Kluge allowed himself a bitter smile. "Let Berlin object. Let them scream. Our job is not to soothe Hitler's paranoia—it's to keep Normandy out of enemy hands."

He walked toward the long windows that looked out over the Seine. Morning mist clung to the fields below. Somewhere beyond those hills, American armor was on the move—Patton's armor, if the reports were accurate. The same general Berlin had mocked for months was now carving through the continent like a sabre through cloth.

Kluge said quietly, "I wonder if Rommel would have seen it coming."

Lang remained silent, knowing better than to offer opinion.

Rommel's absence hung over the room like a shadow. Since being severely wounded in July during a low-level Allied fighter attack, he had been confined to his home in Herrlingen. His voice, once defiant and clear in staff briefings, had fallen silent. Some whispered that he was lucky. Others said he had been removed for knowing too much about the failed July 20th plot. Kluge didn't know which was worse—having Rommel's clarity or bearing his burden alone.

He turned back to the room.

"And Lang—tell the younger staff officers to memorize the word retreat. It may become fashionable again."

August 25, 1944 — 1020 hours

Somewhere inland from Montfarville, Normandy

General George S. Patton Jr. stood in the turret of his command tank, field glasses to his eyes, dust smeared across his face like war paint. The steel walls of the turret reflected morning light, catching flashes of his ivory-handled revolvers at his side.

To the west, smoke plumes spiraled into the sky. Columns of Shermans surged forward through hedgerows, supported by thunderous barrages from Weyland's fighter-bombers overhead. Infantry dashed across wheat fields, ducking beneath the drone of 500-pound bombs descending like the hammer of God.

Patton lowered the glasses.

"Tell Bradley we've cracked the line at Turqueville. I want the 80th pushing south toward Valognes in an hour. And if any son of a bitch so much as hesitates for fuel or maps, they'll find themselves digging latrines from here to Belgium."

His aide snapped a salute and ran off. Patton pulled out a fresh cigar and lit it with trembling fingers.

"They're off balance," he muttered to himself. "This time, we don't stop until the damn Rhine."

Then he smiled grimly.

"Let the bastards in Berlin scream."

August 25, 1944 — 1145 hours

The Reich Chancellery — Berlin

Adolf Hitler's scream tore through the marble corridors of the Chancellery like an artillery blast.

Papers flew from his hand as he surged to his feet from the long war table. His face, already flushed with anger, now turned almost purple. He looked less like a man than a storm about to shatter glass.

"A second invasion?" he shouted, fists clenched and trembling. "They've landed again?! You told me we broke them on June sixth! You swore it!"

General Alfred Jodl remained still, hands folded behind his back. Wilhelm Keitel, his face pale and sweating, opened his mouth—but no sound emerged.

"Four hundred bombers!" Hitler shrieked. "And not one—not one—warning from the Abwehr? Not a whisper from the Luftwaffe? What were you doing—combing sand dunes with a magnifying glass?"

He turned on Keitel, jabbing a trembling finger toward the situation map that now showed markers pushing inland from the Normandy coast.

"You assured me the Atlantic Wall had been reinforced! I gave explicit orders! What happened to the concrete? The bunkers? The mines?"

Keitel cleared his throat. "Mein Führer… Rommel's assessments, after the June engagement, suggested urgent repairs were needed. His staff requested matériel in July—"

"And Rommel," Hitler hissed, "has done nothing since he chose to sunbathe under Allied machine gun fire!"

Jodl said quietly, "Rommel is still recovering from his wounds, mein Führer. OB West is under Field Marshal von Kluge."

Hitler's eyes blazed. "Then Kluge will answer. He was warned. They were all warned!"

He began to pace, one hand clenched behind his back, the other twitching.

"They struck south of Le Havre. That sector was supposed to be under full reinforcement! I gave orders to move reserves—"

"You also gave orders," Jodl interrupted, "to shift armored divisions north toward the Netherlands. We had no divisions to spare."

Hitler spun around. "And now Patton—Patton!—is rampaging through France like a Mongol warlord!"

He leaned against the war table, breath heaving. His fingers clawed at the edge.

"I want Model recalled from the East!" he barked. "Tell him to prepare a thrust from Metz. Move what's left of 2nd SS Panzer south by rail. Strip the Ardennes if you have to. That beachhead must be obliterated!"

Keitel nodded stiffly. "At once, mein Führer."

Hitler turned slowly, eyes locked on the large wall map. Red markers clustered across the Norman coast like infected wounds.

"And Göring?" he asked bitterly.

Jodl said nothing.

Hitler's voice dropped to a rasp. "Tell that fat peacock if he doesn't put a thousand fighters in the air by tomorrow morning, I will personally see to his disgrace. Let him rot in Carinhall with his paintings and his champagne."

He stepped back, jaw clenched.

"They came back," he whispered.

He said it again, more to himself than to anyone in the room. "They came back."

Chapter 27

Kluge in the Thicket

★★★ August 25, 1944 – 1900 Hours. Forward Headquarters — Le Neubourg, France. A damp mist clung to the fading light as it crept across the sodden fields of Normandy. Trees and barns were swallowed by the gray shroud, the quiet broken only by the distant rumble of artillery and the muffled bark of radios inside the commandeered farmhouse. Telephone wires sprawled across the creaking wooden floor like fragile veins, carrying the last pulses of a fading command structure.

Field Marshal Hans Günther von Kluge stood near a tall, warped window, his broad shoulders sagging beneath a weather-stained greatcoat. He had arrived here earlier that afternoon, pushed east from La Roche-Guyon as Patton's advance cracked open the western front. Now the farmstead served as a provisional headquarters for Army Group B—closer to the retreating units, but uncomfortably exposed to enemy airpower.

He had barely eaten. There was no appetite—not with the thunder of war pressing on every side.

Reports streamed in throughout the day, confirming what he already feared: Patton's Shermans had shattered the southern corridor and were moving with stunning speed toward Caen. British and Canadian forces, operating with surgical efficiency, had moved to seal off any axis of retreat, threatening a total encirclement.

He reached toward the table—maps smudged with soot and blood, grease-pencil arrows revised again and again. The command structure beneath him was splintering. Worse, Berlin's delusions hadn't softened since morning—they'd intensified.

"Where is von Luck?" he asked, voice taut as wire.

Major Hellmuth Lang—weary, uniform streaked with sweat and ash—stepped forward. "En route from Vimoutiers, Herr Feldmarschall. His Panzergrenadiers engaged American armor briefly near Écouché but withdrew after sustained air assault. Shermans and Thunderbolts flanked their position."

Kluge's lips curled bitterly. "Withdrawn?"

Lang nodded. "Casualties were light, but morale has begun to fracture. Survivors spoke of napalm. It has left an impression."

The field marshal exhaled sharply and turned toward the glass. Evening mist crawled through the hedgerows, softening the terrain's edges, but not its danger.

"They must hold," Kluge muttered. "Here. Tonight."

He tapped an arc on the map, drawing it from Alençon northward.

"Send orders. Bayerlein's 2nd Panzer Division moves from Alençon now. Fuel shortages be damned. If Patton cuts through Bernay by morning, we lose the Seine."

Lang hesitated. "Berlin is insisting on counteroffensives north of Le Mans—an attempt to split the beachhead, perhaps encircle the British."

Kluge's expression darkened. "Berlin is fighting the war it lost in 1918. They still think war can be managed from a map table."

He leaned over the table, fatigue pressing on his spine. His voice dropped to a gravel whisper: "Delay—that is our only weapon now. Delay, and pray for Allied overreach."

He motioned to a forested sector near Bernay.

"Move the 17th SS Panzergrenadiers into those woods. Mines, booby traps, artillery dug deep. Let Patton find thorns. Bloody thorns."

Lang scratched the directives into his notepad, then paused.

"Herr Feldmarschall... Berlin will not tolerate passive defense."

Kluge's eyes, bloodshot and ringed with shadow, lifted slowly.

"Then let them come to Normandy and hold a shovel."

Silence returned to the farmhouse as Lang departed, his boots echoing on the floorboards.

Kluge remained still. Outside, the mist deepened, cloaking the fields in formless gray. He touched the brim of his field cap.

Though they had never faced one another directly, Kluge had read enough reports from Tunisia and Sicily to understand Patton's methods.

He closed his eyes for a moment, listening—not to the reports or the distant shelling, but to a deeper, darker clock ticking in his mind. A war within the war.

Berlin was watching. Suspicion replaced strategy. Loyalty was now measured in zealotry, not reason.

And Kluge knew: he would not outlive this campaign.

Before the week was out, Model would be summoned to replace him. And Kluge—cornered by Hitler's madness and whispered accusations of treason—would vanish from the war not in battle, but in silence.

Another fracture beneath the eagle.

Victory does not belong to the strongest force—
but to the one that endures the longest moment.

Chapter 28

The Waning Reich

★★★ Berlin – Reich Chancellery. Early September 1944. The rain had begun before dawn, a steady gray drizzle that clung to the soot-stained buildings of Berlin like mourning cloth. The city wore its war fatigue openly now—its stone facades pocked with shrapnel, its gutters choked with fallen leaves and propaganda leaflets, its civilians hollow-eyed beneath the flare of streetlamps. The war had come home—not in bombs, but in silence, in whispered doubts and missing sons.

Inside the Reich Chancellery, the air was heavy with the odor of stale tobacco, damp wool, and the faint metallic tang of fear.

The Führer's private war room—deep in the Chancellery's west wing—was lit not by daylight but by low-hanging brass fixtures that cast golden halos across the dark-paneled walls. Heavy velvet curtains, blood-red and black-lined, remained drawn. The thick burgundy carpet was worn thin by years of pacing boots. At the room's center, a long oak table gleamed under lamplight, its lacquered surface crowded with porcelain teacups, and maps pinned with steel markers.

Adolf Hitler sat slumped at the head of the table, wrapped in a charcoal-gray tunic trimmed with the gold piping of his office. His right arm trembled—more noticeably now than in months past—while his left hand clawed at the armrest. His eyes, bloodshot and shadow-ringed, stared not at the men before him but at the western edge of the wall map behind them, where the Allied push in France had turned from invasion to rout.

He was not the first to speak.

Joseph Goebbels, seated closest to Hitler, leaned forward, his thin frame drawn tighter by the severe lines of his black Propaganda Ministry uniform. His pale fingers drummed lightly on his thigh.

"The news from Normandy is... sobering, mein Führer," he said in a sibilant murmur. "But not irreversible. Our people still believe in you. We must give them something—some symbol of strength. Even now."

Across the table, Hermann Göring shifted, the silver Luftwaffe eagle on his chest catching the light. His blue silk dress uniform strained at the belly, though his cheeks had begun to sag under the weight of sleepless nights and amphetamine withdrawal.

"With all due respect," Göring said, voice bloated with irritation, "the Luftwaffe is strangled. Our pilots are boys. Our fuel is gone. You expect me to hold back American Thunderbolts and British Typhoons with gliders and ghost squadrons?"

Heinrich Himmler, rigid in his black SS uniform adorned with the death's head insignia, said nothing. His round glasses reflected the lamplight, obscuring his eyes. He looked like a crow in human form—cold, patient, waiting to strike.

"Perhaps," he said at last, "the instability in the West is due to... disloyalty among certain generals."

All eyes turned to Martin Bormann, the gray-eyed bureaucrat in an unadorned Wehrmacht field-gray tunic. He wore no medals, but his influence permeated the room. The Führer's gatekeeper, Bormann rarely spoke unless summoned—but his words carried the weight of policy.

"We have reports," he said evenly, "that elements within the Wehrmacht command—some still loyal to the Rommel faction—are advocating a withdrawal from France to consolidate in the interior."

Hitler stirred.

"Rommel is finished," he rasped. "The Canadian airmen did what the courts would not. A traitor neutralized without a trial. There is divine order in that."

He coughed—a dry, papery sound—and flicked his fingers toward the wall map. "Patton has broken through. Our lines unravel. Von Kluge is dead. Rundstedt dithers. Model screams for reinforcements that don't exist. France is bleeding from the jugular, and my generals... my generals would rather bicker and retreat."

No one corrected him. Field Marshal Günther von Kluge had taken poison weeks earlier after his name surfaced in the July 20 plot. Officially, his death was "accidental." No one in the room believed it.

"This is treason by incompetence," Hitler barked, voice rising. "I give orders—they are delayed. Commands—ignored. Watered down like rationed coffee. I should have Rommel's entire staff shot. Not just the ones who signed letters!"

Goebbels leaned forward again, his face pale and taut. "Mein Führer, the people are beginning to ask questions. About the Reich's future. About your health. We must give them confidence."

"Confidence?" Hitler snapped, slamming his fist weakly into the armrest. "Then find me a victory!"

Silence settled like ash.

Outside, thunder rumbled—though it was not thunder, but the distant growl of Allied bombers sweeping over eastern Germany, likely en route to the synthetic oil plants at Leuna or the tank factories at Magdeburg.

Göring shifted again, brow slick with sweat. "If we had fuel—"

"You had your chance, Hermann," Hitler cut in. "Your Luftwaffe is a museum of wreckage."

At the far end of the room, an aide appeared—young, pale, his uniform immaculate—waiting silently until Bormann gave a nod. The boy leaned close and whispered in Bormann's ear.

Bormann straightened, then turned to the Führer. "Message from Army Group B. The Falaise Gap has closed. Nearly fifty thousand men trapped. Entire divisions wiped out. Patton's armor is advancing toward the Seine."

Hitler slumped deeper into his chair, eyes closed, jaw clenched.

The lamplight flickered against the sheen of sweat on his brow.

"Leave me," he whispered. "All of you."

One by one, the men of the Third Reich rose.

Goebbels bowed slightly and backed away. Himmler adjusted his cap, his eyes never leaving Hitler's face. Göring shuffled out, his medals softly clinking. Only Bormann lingered a moment longer—just long enough to catch the look in Hitler's sunken eyes: not only fear, but something else. A glint of the old fanaticism, burning even as the world turned to ash around him.

When the door finally closed, the Führer was alone.

The only sound was the ticking of a wall clock and the soft scratch of rain against the windows.

In the quiet, Hitler looked again at the western edge of the war map. Where once had stood the vision of a fortress Europe, there were now only pins, and crosses, and empty space.

He reached for his teacup, watched his hand tremble again—and let it fall back into his lap.

Chapter 29

Allies and Arrogance

★★★ September 7, 1944 – 0730 Hours. Allied Forward Headquarters, Near Chartres. The tent smelled of sweat, canvas, and damp September grass. Outside, the sun climbed slowly through a veil of early morning mist, casting pale gold over the churned earth and shattered hedgerows of the French countryside. Steel helmets lay forgotten in the grass, German and American alike—mute echoes of the fight that had torn through here days before.

Inside, the real friction was just beginning.

General George S. Patton stood behind the field table, arms folded, jaw locked like iron. The map before him was scarred with grease-pencil thrusts, red arrows driving east across the Seine. But his eyes weren't on the map—they were locked on the man across from him.

Field Marshal Bernard Law Montgomery, crisp in tailored khaki and polished boots, leaned forward just enough to be condescending. His cap rested on the table, regulation-perfect. His every movement, every clipped syllable, carried the self-assurance of a man who believed not only in his authority—but in his infallibility.

"Your advance has been... energetic, General," Montgomery said coolly, eyeing the red lines like they were arterial bleeds. "But you're pushing your flanks too hard. Again."

Patton inhaled, slowly. "You call it energetic. I call it momentum. The Germans didn't expect us to punch back this fast. Now they're off balance—and I intend to keep them that way."

Montgomery arched an eyebrow. "Momentum without coordination becomes recklessness. Your fuel lines are stretched, your infantry is thin, and you're pushing east of Chartres without securing the crossings behind you. That's not strategy, George. That's bravado."

Patton's voice dropped half an octave. "We didn't storm out of Normandy just to crawl into the next province with our heads down. Every hour I wait is another hour Model gets to dig in."

The name landed like a stone between them—General Walter Model, Hitler's newly appointed commander of Army Group B. Ruthless. Quick. And already shifting reinforcements toward the Moselle.

Montgomery's fingers tapped the map. "Model's assembling a defensive screen north of Verdun. You're sprinting straight into his teeth. And if he punches through your side, it won't just be your flank that folds—it'll be the entire Allied axis."

A heavy silence followed. A British colonel coughed near the flap. Patton's aide shifted uncomfortably beside the radio set.

Patton's knuckles whitened on the table edge. "I know who I'm dealing with. And I know how he fights. Model's aggressive—but he's reactive. We've got the sky, we've got the tanks, and for once, we've got them running. I'm not slowing down so the British can catch up in good order."

Montgomery didn't flinch. "This isn't a race. It's a war. Operation Valiant Sword is a coalition effort, not an American cavalry charge."

Patton pointed to the map. "I'm at the Seine. You're still fiddling with pontoons west of Dreux. If that's coalition warfare, Monty, it's running on fumes."

Montgomery's nostrils flared. "The Prime Minister will be informed of your... interpretation."

Patton leaned in, voice low and cold. "Winston asked for victory. Not etiquette."

The tent flap rustled open. A major stepped inside, whispering in Patton's ear. The general's expression tightened.

"Model's shifting armor toward Bernay. He's trying to bottle the corridor before we can cross the Eure."

Montgomery's tone grew clipped. "Then you'll coordinate your strike with the British 21st Army Group. We'll secure your northern shoulder."

Patton narrowed his eyes. "Coordinate, yes. But I'm not slowing down to write love letters. I want Weyland's Thunderbolts on the rail lines by noon, and armor across the river before sunset."

Montgomery rose. "And if your line breaks?"

"Then I'll fix it with fire," Patton said flatly. "And keep going."

Montgomery stood still for a moment longer. The two generals—emblems of the war's two great powers—locked eyes without blinking. Allies by necessity. Rivals by nature.

Finally, Monty turned. "Proceed. But know this—if you overextend and fail, it will stain not only your record, but ours as well."

Patton offered a razor-thin smile. "Then you'd best hope I succeed."

As Montgomery exited into the rising morning light, Patton turned to his aide.

"Get me Weyland on the horn. I want fighter groups strafing those columns and cutting bridges from here to Dreux. If Model wants to shut the door, we're going to blow it off the hinges."

The aide nodded and reached for the radio set.

Patton returned to the map, eyes scanning the line as if daring it to falter. The red arrows ran like rivers toward Metz, toward the Rhine, toward the end of it all.

This time, he told himself, no one's holding me back.

Chapter 30

Flood and Fire

★★★ October 4, 1944 – 1400 Hours. Normandy Interior, South of Montfarville. The roads no longer existed—only churned veins of mud and blood, where wheels, tracks, and boots had ground the French countryside into a graveyard of hedgerows and scorched earth. Patton's Third Army had surged inland faster than anyone thought possible. Barely eight hours after the first Higgins boats kissed sand, his armored columns were ten kilometers deep and still rolling.

General George S. Patton stood in the turret hatch of his command tank—End Run—binoculars pressed to his face, wind tugging at his helmet straps. Ahead, smoke coiled into the October sky from the wreckage of a shattered German convoy. Trucks littered the ditches like toys flung from a child's hand. A Luftwaffe staff car had burned to its frame beneath a crumpled oak, its occupants left slumped and blackened.

He lowered the glasses.

"Send the 4th Armored east," he barked. "Tell 'em to take the crossroads at Saint-Pierre-du-Mont before sundown. If Jerry wants it back, he can fight through Hell to get it."

A radio operator relayed the order with crackling urgency.

Omar Bradley's voice came through the headset a minute later. "George, you sure you're not outrunning your logistics?"

Patton didn't hesitate. "Omar, my tanks eat bullets and piss fire. I'll worry about fuel when I run out of Germans."

He clicked off and turned toward the sloping fields, where infantry picked their way through broken orchard rows. Shermans lumbered past the ruins of a farmhouse still smoldering from a P-47 strike. Each hedgerow was a potential ambush, but resistance had collapsed into chaos—scattered squads, panicked machine-gun nests, and officers deserting in staff cars without orders.

The Wehrmacht hadn't collapsed—it had cracked. And Patton intended to keep hammering until it shattered.

He leaned toward his driver. "Get us to Forward CP Alpha. I want to hear from Hillman with my own ears. No more radio hopscotch."

The tank groaned forward. Overhead, three Thunderbolts banked low in formation, dropping napalm across the treeline. The blast rolled across the fields in a wave of light and noise, setting whole acres ablaze. Somewhere, a German squad died in that fire, unseen.

At the chapel-turned-command post, Patton dismounted. Major Hillman stood beneath the shattered altar, scrawling orders across a map balanced on a crate of .30-caliber rounds.

"You're pressing the line hard," Hillman said with a salute. "Third Battalion reached Amfreville Ridge. They spotted armor retreating—possibly a Tiger company, but they didn't fire. Looked like they were fleeing."

"Running?" Patton repeated. "Good. Chase them. Don't let them regroup. No sleep tonight."

He stabbed the map with a grease pencil. "That hamlet—east of Caen—controls the valley road. We take it, we split their axis of retreat. Weyland's air controllers are riding our lead Shermans. Ask, and ye shall receive."

Hillman nodded. "The British are behind us. Advancing, but slow."

Patton's grin turned sour. "Montgomery's marching to the rhythm of a funeral dirge."

He stepped outside. Sunlight filtered red through smoke pillars, casting everything in the hue of war. Along the road, half-tracks rolled past, engines growling. Civilians waved from broken stone gates. A boy held up a hand-painted flag and screamed, "Liberté!" as a GI tossed him a Hershey bar.

It felt unstoppable.

Then came the Jeep. It skidded to a halt, tires throwing gravel. A courier jumped out and thrust a sealed envelope into Colonel Gaffey's hands.

Patton approached, his boots cracking dried mud. "What is it?"

Gaffey opened it, read it, then paled. "General... it's from SHAEF."

Patton snatched the message and scanned it twice, his jaw tightening.

ALL FORCES OF THIRD ARMY ARE TO HOLD
PRESENT POSITIONS EFFECTIVE IMMEDIATELY.
NO ADVANCE TO BE MADE TOWARD PARIS
UNTIL FURTHER ORDERS.

His voice dropped to a growl. "What the hell is this?"

"Orders from Eisenhower," Gaffey said. "Came down the pipe two hours ago."

Patton dismounted. The rumble of engines faded in his ears as his rage rose to fill the space. He looked east—toward Paris. Barely forty miles. He could almost hear the bells of Notre-Dame. And now this?

"Get me Bradley. Now."

Minutes later, in his mobile command truck, he barked into the field set. "Omar, don't give me this crap. I've got gas, I've got men, and I've got Jerry in full retreat."

Bradley's voice was subdued. "George, the orders are real. Direct from Ike. Politics are in play—De Gaulle, Leclerc, Churchill... and the Soviets are watching."

Patton slammed the handset down.

Outside, the men were still loading, still rolling. Paris was expecting them. Civilians lined the roads, waving and weeping. A girl offered flowers to a passing column. A priest knelt beside a field hospital tent, blessing the wounded.

That evening, under a canvas canopy, Patton sat at his map table, staring at the names: Chartres. Dreux. Versailles. Paris.

He wrote to his wife:

The hardest battles are not always fought with bullets, but with silence.

By dawn, another dispatch arrived. This one more personal.

REPORT TO SUPREME HEADQUARTERS IN
LONDON. TRAVEL IMMEDIATELY.

Patton crushed the page in his gloved hand.

"Tell Gaffey he's got the army till I return. And tell him to keep the engines warm."

He looked one last time toward the northeast. Fog blanketed the horizon, hiding the spires of Paris. Behind the mist lay a city begging for liberation.

And politics had chained his advance.

Chapter 31

The Halt Before Paris

★★★ The twin engines of the C-47 transport groaned as it banked low across the English Channel, wings slicing the salt-laced air. General George S. Patton sat strapped into a canvas seat, silent, jaw clenched like granite. He hadn't spoken since lifting off from the Normandy airstrip. His eyes stayed fixed on the horizon, but his mind roamed the fields of France—still storming the crossroads, chasing Tigers, and reaching for the gates of Paris.

Two P-51 Mustangs flanked the transport on one wing. On the other, two P-47 Thunderbolts shadowed them at a slight offset, wings gleaming silver in the high light. Escort or tribute? Patton couldn't tell. He didn't care.

Southern England emerged in the distance like a painting taking shape—mist swirling above fields quilted in green and gold, scattered villages beginning to stir under a hesitant sun. RAF Northolt shimmered below, its runways dry and orderly, in sharp contrast to the churned mud of Normandy. On the tarmac, a polished black staff car waited, bearing the unmistakable SHAEF insignia.

When Patton stepped off the ramp, British ground personnel straightened. They didn't salute—wrong protocol—but their posture told another story. Recognition. Respect. Perhaps even awe.

The drive into London passed without a word. Streets were crowded but subdued. Civilians paused as the staff car rolled past. A woman in widow's black pressed a gloved hand to her chest. A small boy lifted his arm in a sharp salute, eyes wide. The legend had arrived, and even the city seemed to hold its breath.

At Grosvenor Square—the heartbeat of Allied High Command—Patton was led through a maze of polished corridors. He was ushered into a chamber that felt more like a gentlemen's club than a war room. No buzz of field telephones here. No urgent clatter of typewriters. Only the hush of decision-making power. Maps hung in gilded frames. Crystal ashtrays overflowed with crushed cigars. Tobacco smoke clung to the drapes, the rugs, the very air.

General George C. Marshall stood when Patton entered. Beside him, Admiral William D. Leahy nodded, face unreadable. The seat at the end of the long table—Eisenhower's—remained empty.

"General Patton," Marshall said, offering his hand. "Welcome to London."

Patton took it. "General. Admiral."

"You've done the impossible," Leahy said. "Again."

Marshall gestured to a leather chair. "You've turned the tide of the war, George. And done it faster than anyone thought possible. The President is grateful."

Patton lowered himself into the seat without ceremony. "Then why am I here instead of in Paris?"

Marshall leaned forward, elbows resting on the table. "Because war isn't just bullets and tanks anymore. It's politics now. And what comes after."

He slid a folder across the polished wood. Patton opened it. Inside were official papers: promotion to four-star general, another Silver Star, and a citation written in language too elegant to be battlefield-born.

To Patton, it felt like a velvet muzzle.

Leahy's voice softened. "This isn't just a military campaign anymore. It's a chess match. Ike's been chosen to play the next phase. He's acceptable to Churchill. And Stalin."

"And I'm not," Patton said, his tone flat.

"You're a sword," Marshall replied evenly. "Not a scalpel. But we need the sword, too."

Patton closed the folder. His hand rested on it a moment longer than necessary.

"I'm returning to the front?"

"With full command," Marshall said. "The Germans aren't finished. Not yet. When they counterattack—and they will—we'll want you waiting."

Patton stood. His cape swept behind him as he turned. "Tell Eisenhower," he said without venom, "to try and keep up."

No further words were spoken.

He walked out of the chamber and into the corridor. The young officers lining the hall parted without a word. No applause. No cheers. Just silence. Reverence. As though thunder itself had walked past.

Patton didn't look back. He didn't need to. He already knew where he was going.

There was no time for politics.

The war was calling.

Chapter 32
The Watchers at Herrlingen

★★★ Herrlingen, Germany — Early October 1944. Villa Lindenhof, the Rommel Residence. The house at Herrlingen lay nestled among ancient oaks and chestnut trees of the Swabian Jura, a steep, wooded land where autumn arrived with curling mists and the smell of chimney smoke. The Villa Lindenhof stood modest and dignified behind its wrought-iron gate, its pale stone walls softening beneath ivy and the weight of morning fog.

It might have seemed peaceful.

But it was not.

Inside, the air was heavy and still—muffled, as if the house had become a shrine. Every sound was hushed, absorbed by thick rugs and closed doors, as though even the walls knew that something sacred—or tragic—was nearing its end.

Upstairs, in a second-floor bedroom behind white lace curtains, Field Marshal Erwin Rommel lay propped against pillows, pale as the linen beneath him.

The once-formidable Desert Fox—his skin bronzed by North African sun, his jaw squared with command—was now diminished. His head remained wrapped in bandages from the cranial injury he'd sustained in the Spitfire attack outside Sainte-Foy-de-Montgommery. Beneath the gauze, a silver scar traced his right temple, disappearing into thinning hair. Though conscious and occasionally lucid, he was frail, often dizzy, and hypersensitive to light.

Beside him, Lucie Rommel sat in silence, knitting in her lap, though her fingers rarely moved. More often, her eyes remained fixed on the window. Their sixteen-year-old son Manfred, temporarily released from his Hitler Youth academy, sat nearby pretending to read. But every so often, his gaze flicked to his father's face, watching for movement—for breath.

Downstairs, the quiet footsteps were not those of servants.

They belonged to plainclothes SS officers.

They had arrived discreetly in the week following Rommel's return from the Ulm military hospital. Officially, they were there to "protect the national hero"—a man admired by soldiers and civilians alike, a figurehead of discipline in a regime teetering between delusion and collapse.

Unofficially, they were there to watch.

To listen.

To isolate.

Rommel, though weakened, remained dangerous—not for what he had done, but for what others believed he might do. After the failed July 20 assassination attempt on Hitler, investigators found traces of Rommel's peripheral knowledge. He had opposed assassination, yes, but he had also lost faith. He had told friends the Reich needed a negotiated peace.

To the SS, that was treason enough.

On the second Thursday of October, SS-Sturmbannführer Wilhelm Weitz stood near the hearth in Rommel's study. He wore civilian clothes, but his ramrod posture and cold efficiency betrayed his rank. Across from him sat Dr. Hans Speidel, Rommel's former chief of staff—one of the few visitors permitted to call. Speidel sipped from a porcelain cup he never brought fully to his lips.

"The Field Marshal is progressing," Speidel said evenly. "He sat upright for twenty minutes this morning."

Weitz gave a pleasant nod. "That is good news. Berlin remains concerned for his well-being."

Speidel's tone cooled. "And yet, he is a prisoner in all but name."

Weitz offered a faint smile, as if the idea amused him. "You misunderstand, Doctor. The Reich simply wishes to ensure the safety of its most revered general. There are... unsavory elements who might seek to exploit his good name. We must protect him from that."

Speidel said nothing. He knew better than to argue with euphemisms.

Upstairs, Rommel stirred. He could hear the murmuring voices through the floorboards—Weitz, no doubt, with his suffocating veneer of politeness. He shifted slightly and winced. A cool cloth pressed against his brow—Lucie's hand. Her presence, as always, unwavering.

He had no illusions.

He remembered the fate of General von Witzleben. The coerced suicides of Ludwig Beck and Friedrich Olbricht. Even Field Marshal Kluge—so loyal, so careful—had swallowed poison.

Rommel had once served Hitler with conviction. He had believed in the energy of the man, if not his ideology. But Africa had opened his eyes. France had broken his spirit. And the July bomb had convinced him that Germany's soul was bleeding to death—one lie at a time.

He turned his head, fighting the dizziness, and looked at Lucie.

"I don't think they will let me live much longer," he said quietly.

She didn't speak. Her eyes shimmered but stayed dry. She only reached down and took his hand, gripping it tighter.

Outside, a dark gray Opel Kapitän idled in the gravel drive, its exhaust curling like a snake in the morning air. Two SS men sat inside, rifles cradled across their laps, eyes fixed forward.

Another day of watching. Another day of waiting.

For the order that might never come—or that might come tonight.

Chapter 33
The Final Order

★★★ Herrlingen, Germany — October 14, 1944. Villa Lindenhof, early morning mist. A low fog blanketed the Swabian hills, draping the wooded slopes like mourning cloth. Dew clung to every blade of grass and silvered the branches of the old oaks that lined the roads. The mist moved slowly, almost reverently, as if even nature paused to hold its breath. Not a bird sang. The familiar rustle of the hedgerows was absent. Only the distant rhythm of a freight train, groaning toward Ulm, broke the silence.

Inside the Rommel household, the quiet was heavier still.

Lucie Rommel stood at the kitchen window, her hands resting on the edge of the sink, a dishcloth forgotten in her grip. Her face, once spirited and full of light, was drawn and pale. Fine lines etched her cheeks like soft scars from too many sleepless nights. Behind her, a pot of weak coffee simmered untouched on the stove. The faint aroma mingled with the scent of damp leaves and ash from last night's fire.

Upstairs, Field Marshal Erwin Rommel sat at his writing desk, dressed with meticulous care in his full field uniform. Field-gray tunic pressed smooth, silver piping crisp at the collar, Knight's Cross shining beneath his throat. His Afrika Korps cap rested neatly on the nearby armchair, a remnant of brighter days under harsher suns.

He knew.

He had known for days.

The watchers had become quieter. More deferential. Their orders more exact. And then came the message—two generals were arriving from Berlin, emissaries from the Führer himself: General Wilhelm Burgdorf and General Ernst Maisel. "Personal business," they said.

Rommel stared into the cold fire in the hearth. It had been lit that morning for appearance, not warmth. On the desk lay several papers he no longer had the strength to finish. A half-written letter to Manfred. A note to Lucie, the pen strokes faint and unfinished.

His left hand rested flat on the polished wood, trembling slightly.

The knock came precisely at 11:00.

The butler, grave and silent, led the two officers into the study. Burgdorf entered first—tall, hard-featured, his expression carved from stone. Maisel followed, shorter, more somber, eyes never rising to meet Rommel's.

Rommel stood slowly, every motion deliberate. His bearing remained that of a soldier to the end—dignified, alert, unflinching.

"Gentlemen," he said, his voice even.

"Field Marshal," Burgdorf replied with a clipped nod.

They took their seats without preamble. No handshakes. No formalities. The silence between them was not awkward—it was ancient.

Lucie lingered just beyond the doorway, watching through the narrow crack. Her hand gripped the stair rail with such force her knuckles whitened.

Burgdorf began. "Herr Feldmarschall, I come bearing a message from the Führer. A matter of national urgency."

Rommel said nothing. His face, composed and implacable, gave no hint of surprise. Only the shadows under his eyes betrayed the fatigue of months spent in slow exile.

"You are accused of complicity in the July 20 plot," Burgdorf continued. "While definitive evidence is lacking, testimonies suggest you were aware of the plan. Others have denied it. Some have named you."

Rommel's lips parted slightly. "And the Führer's decision?"

Maisel, more cautious, took over. "You are to be given a choice. The Führer recognizes your service to the Reich. You will be granted a full military funeral. Your rank and honors preserved. Your family spared any consequence."

A pause.

"Or," Burgdorf said with finality, "you will be tried in the People's Court for high treason. Your name condemned. Your family... punished. The Gestapo is prepared to act."

The air in the room thickened.

Rommel's gaze drifted upward to the photo on the mantel—an old image from the desert campaign. He stood in sunlight then, goggles slung around his neck, the laughter of comrades just out of frame. A different time. A different man.

"How long do I have?" he asked quietly.

Burgdorf reached into his coat and placed a small wooden box on the desk. The hinges creaked slightly as he opened it—inside, a single glass vial with a white capsule. Cyanide.

"Ten minutes," Burgdorf said. "We will wait in the car."

They rose and departed. The door clicked shut behind them.

Lucie entered immediately. Her eyes searched his, her mouth trembling. "They gave you the poison."

Rommel nodded once.

Tears welled in her eyes, but she fought them. "Let me bring Manfred."

"No," Rommel said firmly, taking her hand. "Not yet. He should remember me... as I was. Not like this. He is too young to carry this weight."

Lucie turned away, her shoulders trembling. "This is murder."

Rommel looked at her. "It's mercy. Dressed in a uniform."

He kissed her hand gently, lingered there. Then rose, adjusted his cap before the mirror, straightening it with soldier's precision.

"I have fought for Germany all my life," he murmured. "But this... this is my final command. One last act of discipline. Of protection."

Lucie caressed his face. "You don't have to do this."

"I do," he replied softly. "To protect you. And Manfred. That's all I have left."

Outside, the Opel Admiral idled at the gate, exhaust curling like smoke from a funeral pyre. The mist had thickened. Burgdorf and Maisel stood at attention by the car, their eyes fixed on the gravel drive.

Rommel gave Lucie one last look. No fear. Only resolve.

Then he stepped out into the mist.

They drove a short distance, away from the village, to a clearing beneath tall fir trees. There were no witnesses. No escorts. Just Rommel, the two generals, and the silence of a secluded wood.

He asked to be alone.

They gave him the wooden box and stepped back.

He stood briefly beside the stone bench near the roadside clearing, the autumn air cool against his face. The wooded hills around Herrlingen were silent beneath the gray October sky. Burgdorf waited nearby, rigid and expressionless, while the driver remained at the wheel of the staff car. Rommel said nothing more. After a final glance toward the trees, he climbed quietly into the back seat beside General Maisel.

The car pulled away slowly beneath the canopy of oaks. Several minutes later, Rommel removed the cyanide capsule hidden in his tunic. There was no struggle, no final declaration. Only a tightening of his jaw and a sudden change in his breathing as the poison took hold. By the time the staff car turned toward Ulm, the Field

Marshal had collapsed against the seat, dying within minutes as the stunned occupants watched in silence.

Africa. The long roads of France. The camaraderie. The lost men. No general ever commanded his own death. Until now.

Later that evening, Berlin announced the tragic death of Field Marshal Erwin Rommel, attributing it to complications from his wounds. The nation mourned. A hero, they said, had succumbed to war's invisible injuries. A state funeral was promised. Flags lowered.

But in Villa Lindenhof, only silence remained.

And in the hearts of Lucie, Manfred, and a few men with unclouded eyes, the truth endured.

They never forgot the quiet morning when the Reich silenced its most honorable soldier.

Chapter 34

Frozen Valor

★★★ The roads through the Ardennes gleamed with frost, slick and narrow as they wound through shadowed forest hills. Patton's staff car sliced through the biting wind, tires crunching over gravel edged with ice. Bare branches stretched like skeletal fingers against a pale winter sky, their limbs etched in silver frost. The war had slowed—its wild momentum drained by cold and caution.

Gone was the breakneck charge across France, replaced now by a tense stillness, the front line frozen just short of the German border. The Wehrmacht had not fallen; it had only pulled back, waiting. And Patton, restless and watchful, knew the fight was far from over.

At his field headquarters near Nancy, Patton paced like a coiled spring. The Third Army—his army—sat idling, its drive sapped by new orders and the slow creep of Allied bureaucracy.

"We're feeding them time," he snarled to General Hobart Gay. "Give the enemy time, and they'll strike back. Hard."

Harder than anyone expected.

On December 16, the forests exploded. German panzers burst from the mist, smashing into fragile American lines across Belgium and Luxembourg. Hitler's desperate gamble—the Ardennes counteroffensive—had begun.

The front fractured. Entire regiments scattered like leaves in a gale. Bastogne, a small, seemingly unimportant crossroads in peacetime, suddenly became everything. Whoever held Bastogne held the roads—and the roads, in winter, were life itself.

Inside the town, the 101st Airborne Division and elements of the 10th Armored were surrounded. Seven German divisions—including the elite Panzer Lehr—encircled the frozen defenders. With planes grounded by weather and supply lines cut, foxholes became graves, and the forest itself seemed to close in.

Major Richard "Dick" Winters, of Easy Company, 506th PIR, paced a shallow trench west of town. The battered remnants of his men clung to their weapons like lifelines. Shells shrieked overhead. The night sky pulsed red with artillery flashes.

He turned to Lieutenant Buck Compton, who was wrapping his bleeding hand with a strip of parachute silk.

"Still think we're gonna get that Christmas pass, Buck?" Winters asked, a thin grin cutting through the cold.

Compton exhaled, vapor curling from his lips. "Only if Santa's driving a Sherman."

In the command post beneath Bastogne's town hall, Brigadier General Anthony McAuliffe studied a map littered with pins and ink. When a German envoy arrived on the morning of December 22 with a demand for surrender, McAuliffe stared at the typed ultimatum and then muttered the word that would enter history.

"Nuts."

The message was delivered. The lines held.

At an emergency meeting in a commandeered château at Verdun, the Allied high command gathered, the air thick with urgency. Patton studied the map in near silence—red markers bleeding deep into Allied territory.

Eisenhower looked directly at him. "George, how soon can you get north?"

Patton's answer came swift, fierce: "We're already moving."

A stunned silence followed.

"We've been planning for a German breakout for weeks," Patton said, voice low and steady. "I can swing three divisions ninety degrees in forty-eight hours."

The plan sounded impossible.

But Patton made it happen.

The 4th Armored Division, 26th Infantry Division, and 80th Infantry Division wheeled northeast. Through blizzards and blackouts, columns of Shermans thundered north, headlights dimmed, engines howling against frozen climbs. Soldiers rode in open halftracks, faces windburned, gloves frozen stiff on rifles. Chaplains recited psalms over radios. Medics patched wounds with numb hands. The Third Army surged forward, fierce and relentless.

On December 26, Patton's spearhead reached the outskirts of Bastogne. The siege was broken from the south. The defenders had held, fueled not by rations or reinforcements but by grit.

From a frostbitten ridgeline overlooking the battered town, Patton stared through snow and smoke.

"They held," he said quietly. "Now we finish it."

In the days that followed, the Third Army ripped apart German flanks. Villages were wrested from SS fanatics, convoys turned to wreckage, and forest trails clogged with abandoned tanks. Bastogne became legend—a symbol of American defiance—and so did the general who brought relief.

But no parades awaited Patton. No front-page banner headlines in New York or London. The cold politics of command simmered beneath the victory. Eisenhower remained the public face. Montgomery the British counterweight. Patton, for all his brilliance, remained the blunt edge—effective but unruly, admired but unwelcome at the negotiating table.

Back at headquarters, he paced the floorboards as a fire sputtered in the hearth.

On New Year's Day, he wrote in his diary:

"I fought the war they needed, but not the war they wanted. Let the historians sort it out. My men and I—we were ready."

The Battle of the Bulge had been his last great maneuver. His final test of steel. It proved that even in the bitterest cold, American resolve burned hot enough to melt the enemy's grip.

But Patton was far from done.

As snow gave way to mud in January 1945, the Third Army pushed east again. Through ruined hamlets and shattered forests, the Saar Basin loomed ahead—a fortress of factories and concrete defenses buried within the Siegfried Line. Eisenhower urged caution. Patton heard it as a challenge.

"We've cracked bigger nuts than this," he muttered to Gay, pointing at a smudged map of Saarbrücken. "They said Bastogne was suicide too."

In February, artillery thundered through the valleys. Tanks rolled forward into cratered towns. House by house, mile by mile, the Third Army forced the enemy back.

Resistance was brutal. SS units ambushed from cellars. Hitler Youth fired Panzerfausts from church windows. But nothing stopped Patton.

In March, they reached the Rhine—not at Remagen, where headlines hailed a lucky crossing, but farther south, near Oppenheim. Engineers built pontoon bridges under darkness and fire. Patton stood on the west bank, watching a Sherman lead the charge.

He lit a cigar and grinned.

"I don't wait for permission," he said. "I wait for opportunity."

Germany unraveled. Hitler raged in his bunker, issuing phantom orders. Patton cut through Bavaria like a sword.

Cities fell like dominoes—Würzburg, Aschaffenburg, Nuremberg.

Where torchlight rallies once stirred zealotry, now silence hung beneath crumbling eagles.

With liberation came horror.

In April, the Third Army found Ohrdruf—the first Nazi concentration camp uncovered by the Western Allies. Emaciated prisoners—many of them Jews—stared through hollow eyes as American soldiers moved through the camp in stunned silence. Patton entered the gates and nearly collapsed. Outside the compound, he vomited behind a half-track.

Later, he forced local officials to walk the camp.

"You lived next to this," he shouted. "You breathed this air. Now you look."

He wrote in his journal:

"I never thought men could sink so low. If we allow this to be forgotten, we deserve no peace."

That memory haunted him more than any battlefield.

By late April, the Third Army pushed into Austria. Rumors swirled of Nazi fanatics hiding in alpine redoubts. Patton meant to flush them out.

"I'll smoke them out of every cave from here to Innsbruck," he barked.

On May 4, his lead tanks rolled into Linz.

In the shadow of the mountains, the Reich crumbled. White flags replaced gunfire. Officers wept, saluted, surrendered trembling pistols.

On May 8, 1945—Victory in Europe Day—Germany surrendered.

Patton did not attend any grand ceremony.

At a field hospital near Regensburg, he knelt beside a young corporal who had lost both legs to a mine.

"Did we win, sir?" the boy whispered.

Patton took his hand.

"Yes, son. You won it for all of us."

That evening, as the Danube glimmered under a golden dusk, Patton sat alone.

No parades. No fanfare.

Just silence—and the ache of a war he wasn't ready to leave behind.

In his diary, he wrote:

"This was the war I was made for. And now that it's done, I find myself without a war to fight. But I'll be damned if I let the peace unravel what the war had forged in blood and fire."

The war in Europe was over.

But for George S. Patton, the peace loomed—strange, political, and far more elusive than war.

War does not begin when the first shot is fired. It begins long before—in the quiet certainty that it must.

Epilogue

Cartographers of Consequence

★★★ The war had not ended. But something else had—certainty, perhaps. The world now moved beneath a darker sky, its horizons refracted through smoke and disillusionment. Plans once etched in confidence had turned to ash. Convictions that had steeled armies were now tempered by loss. A single failed June had reshaped the global order—not with surrender, but with suspicion.

The age of consequence had begun.

In the East, Soviet tanks clawed through the summer wheatfields of Belarus, their steel hulls streaked with mud, scorched by artillery, and worn by relentless advance. Operation Bagration, once designed to strike in tandem with a Western offensive, now bore the full brunt of Hitler's rage alone. Entire villages were flattened. Marshes turned to charnel grounds. The Red Army pressed forward, inch by agonizing inch, but trust in its Western partners had withered.

In the Politburo, maps were redrawn not with vision, but with vengeance. Patience gave way to paranoia. Diplomats whispered of betrayal.

And Stalin—never quick to forgive—began to imagine borders not as lines of defense, but as buffer zones carved from the weakness of others.

In the West, the smoke had cleared from the forests of Luxembourg.

On a frozen ridge overlooking the Moselle Valley, General George S. Patton stood with one gloved hand on his hip, wind tugging at his trench coat like a restless spirit. Below him, the battlefield lay hushed—no artillery, no machine gun chatter. Just churned snow, rusting metal, and the echo of what had nearly been catastrophe.

The Ardennes counteroffensive had been repelled—barely.

Patton's Third Army, summoned like a storm, had moved with blistering speed through snow-choked roads, encircling German spearheads, rescuing trapped divisions, and punching holes through elite Panzer regiments. His men had broken the siege at Bastogne. They had done what others could not.

And yet, even victory bore teeth.

"I was sent to clean up a mess," he told a war correspondent with a scowl. "Not to be anyone's savior. I don't believe in salvation."

For the first time since Sicily, Patton's name moved through Washington not with contempt—but with calculation. Congressmen spoke of his 'clarity.' Generals debated his recklessness less and his results more. He had become, however reluctantly, a weapon America might need again.

At the White House, Franklin Roosevelt sat alone in the Oval Office. The lamps were low. A fire sputtered quietly in the grate.

On his desk lay an opened letter—another grieving mother asking a question for which there was no proper answer: "Why did my son die in Normandy?"

His reply had already been drafted, its tone measured, its phrases refined with the weary precision of a man who had written too many like it:

He died in the service of a free world still being born. His sacrifice lives in the lives it will protect.

Roosevelt read it again, then placed it back into the pile. He knew it wasn't enough. How could it be? What sentence could stand against a son's absence at the dinner table forever?

Outside, the nation turned uncertain eyes toward November. Roosevelt had weathered political collapse, military disaster, and waves of public grief. Some now called him stubborn. Others, decisive. Most simply waited to see if the man who had led them through the Depression could still lead them through this darker valley.

In his final campaign speech before the election, Roosevelt did not offer promises. He offered grit.

"This war is not a storybook," he said, voice rasping with illness. "It is not scripted, and it is not fair. But we are still here. Still fighting. Still free."

Across the Atlantic, Winston Churchill stood before a restless Parliament, his knuckles white on the dispatch box. His shoulders seemed heavier now, the fire of 1940 dulled but not gone.

Normandy's failure had nearly toppled his government. The Conservative benches had whispered mutiny. Labour ministers had sharpened questions like blades. And yet, it was Patton's winter charge through Belgium that had thrown him a lifeline.

"History," Churchill said, voice thick with gravel and gravitas, "will not remember us for one stormy June. But for what we did after the tide turned."

There was no eruption of applause. But neither was there a motion of no confidence.

For now, the lion endured.

And in Germany—where silence now cloaked the ruins more thickly than ash—no monument stood for Erwin Rommel.

He had died as he had lived in his final days—caught between duty and conscience. Once the Desert Fox, a symbol of German military prowess untainted by Nazi fanaticism, Rommel had become a liability to the Reich—a man too popular, too principled, too dangerous.

After being implicated in the failed plot to assassinate Hitler, he was given a choice: stand trial and see his family disgraced, or take his own life and be buried with full military honors.

He chose silence.

The Nazi regime announced to the public that Rommel had succumbed to wounds sustained in Normandy weeks earlier—injuries from an airstrike on his staff car. Newspapers printed tributes. State funerals were arranged. But no truth accompanied the ceremony.

The story was a lie, dutifully told, and carefully rehearsed.

Yet across Europe, the truth seeped through cracks in the façade. Resistance fighters passed it in whispers. Allied officers spoke of it in briefings. Civilians scribbled his name beside the word Verräter—traitor—or Held—hero.

And on the walls of ruined cities and railway stations in occupied France, someone scrawled:

Rommel lebt. Die Wahrheit stirbt nie.

Rommel lives. Truth never dies.

It was not a tribute to the man alone, but to the idea that somewhere within even the darkest machinery of war, there had once been a voice that said no.

In Washington, London, and Moscow, cartographers bent over broad tables, their eyes red with fatigue.

They inked new borders, plotted next offensives, calculated acceptable losses. But no map could capture the shift that had taken root in the soul of civilization.

Because Normandy's failure had not just claimed lives.

It had cost the illusion that the war was inevitable—or winnable by virtue alone. It had reminded the world that history, like war, is built not by destiny, but by desperate men in brutal weather. And it had exposed the frailty of alliances, the limits of resolve, the price of delay.

And yet, still, they drew their lines.

And still, men crossed them.

Author's Note

General George S. Patton remains one of history's most compelling and complex figures—a brilliant strategist, a fierce warrior, and a man whose unyielding nature has sparked both admiration and controversy. This narrative seeks to honor his remarkable military achievements while candidly acknowledging the personal and political struggles that shaped his legacy.

The events chronicled here are grounded in extensive historical research, drawing from firsthand accounts, official records, and the reflections of those who fought alongside him. Yet beyond the grand sweep of history lies a profoundly human story—a story of courage, ambition, sacrifice, and the enduring search for meaning in the aftermath of war.

My own fascination with Patton's life grew from the tension between his battlefield brilliance and his deeply human flaws. It is this balance that I hoped to bring to light—a portrait not just of a general, but of a man shaped by the tumultuous forces of his time.

Thank you for joining me on this journey through one of the pivotal chapters of the twentieth century. May the lessons of valor, resilience, and humanity continue to inspire and challenge us all.

Frank W. Edwards
Glendale, Arizona

Acknowledgements

I would like to express my sincere appreciation to Eddie Atkinson for his careful work in the formatting and presentation of this manuscript. His experience, patience, and attention to detail have been invaluable throughout this process.

www.ingramcontent.com/pod-product-compliance
Lightning Source LLC
LaVergne TN
LVHW020719110826
845149LV00012B/2327

* 9 7 8 1 9 7 0 7 9 8 0 6 7 *